Ice Cold Lover
By Mel Teshco

Ice Cold Lover
By Mel Teshco
Text copyright © 2015 Mel Teshco
All Rights Reserved

This one's for all the gargoyle fans. Thanks for loving my series

Cover Art by Kellie Dennis at Book Cover by Design
www.bookcoverbydesign.co.uk[1]

---

1. http://www.bookcoverbydesign.co.uk

Chapter One

The smell of money, and lots of it, permeated the air of the Sydney casino as Celeste Diamond stepped out of the elevator and onto its lavish third floor. Booked exclusively for invitation-only guests, it was here the rich and powerful, the famous and not-so-famous, came to flaunt their splendor.

She scarcely noticed. Instead, every one of her senses isolated the man who'd gone to great lengths this last month—with little success—to get to know her.

Pascal Daniels was a name synonymous to power and wealth, with murky undercurrents linking him to the seedy underworld of organized crime. Add notorious playboy to the mix and he was one black sheep she'd do well to avoid—if only she wasn't a heartbeat away from tearing the clothes right off his magnificent body!

Heat crept up her throat as high-voltage lust zapped straight between her thighs. Her nipples pebbled beneath her white sheath dress and the corset bra under the many layers of gauzy material encircling her torso.

Pascal would never see the physical evidence puckering just for him. The corset disguised more than just her gargoyle wings.

She watched him push to his feet in one smooth, fluid movement. He towered above the blackjack table and a pair of scantily clad women who'd been hanging over him. He ignored them both. Instead, his hot stare feasted on her, swept her up and down like a lover's caress, his attention hers alone.

She swallowed convulsively. When he abandoned his chips with a careless wave, the breath wedged somewhere low in her throat.

Oh, dear god. Am I ready for this?

Her spine snapped tight, subduing the hideous, bat-like appendages quivering beneath their bonds. And for just one moment self-doubt iced the carnal heat flowing like lava in her veins. Would this man be so fascinated if he saw her in all her naked glory, with her unbound wings stretched high and wide?

She'd never give him the chance to find out.

Oh, they'd be intimate this night, except it would be strictly on her terms, when she was ready and not before. She would never be one of his easy conquests.

With slow provocation, she turned her back on him, a gesture that made her shiver even as she burned. Had anyone ever had the nerve to snub this man?

Snatching a flute of champagne from a passing tray, she sipped the bubbles of decadence while dancing her way around the milling crowd of glitterati. She needn't look behind to see if he followed—her every molecule screamed that he did. A gurgle of laughter spilled free, a dizzy excitement from the thrill of the hunt. She hadn't felt so alive, so utterly aroused...ever!

Pascal had awakened something deep inside her, unleashed needs that weren't just physical. He'd stimulated her mentally too. Though she'd kept any dialogue between them brief, she'd discovered a man incredibly complex and intelligent.

A man wholly in control.

"Celeste!" Over the buzz of conversation, the throaty voice of her friend, Lexie, was unmistakable. The dark-haired woman motioned her over to where she was placing bets at a roulette wheel. "I wondered if you would make it," she said with a mock glower, leaning toward her and air kissing each cheek.

Celeste inwardly grimaced, her joy evaporating. Even acquaintances knew better than to touch her. It hurt to know they all imagined her "no-touch policy" was used solely to cultivate her ice-queen image.

They couldn't be more wrong.

"I couldn't resist," she conceded wryly. Then sweeping a look at Lexie's double stack of chips, she murmured, "You're on a winning streak."

Her friend grinned, shamelessly blasé as she swept out a languid, heavily bejeweled hand. "Not at all. I've lost almost everything I came here with."

With Lexie's family owning shipping lines and major foreign media shares, Celeste supposed her friend could afford to be careless. Her lips pursed. One day she'd have that conversation with her about using money in a more altruistic way.

Sudden heat prickled along her nape, blasting philosophical thoughts clean away. Her pulse thudded, every one of her muscles tensing in reaction. Pascal had come to claim her.

Lexie's grin widened, and then became predatory as she peered past her and arched a thinly-plucked brow. "Well, Little Miss Secretive," Lexie turned a speculative gaze her way, "I suspect you won't be going home a loser tonight."

Celeste recognized thinly veiled jealousy when she heard it but didn't rise to the bait. Still, she couldn't help but turn to face the man who'd invaded her dreams and morphed them into something deliciously wicked for twenty-six nights straight.

"Good evening, ladies," Pascal murmured, his husky voice as smooth and fine as a long sip of aged malt whiskey.

Lexie preened, unmistakably a pushover for this man with his handsome face, athlete's body and a charisma that beckoned at twenty paces. Add to his repertoire oodles of charm, power and wealth, and Celeste could almost empathize.

"Mind if I steal your friend?" Pascal asked the dark-haired woman.

"Oh, I'm sure she won't mind," Lexie purred. "It's not as if she's here to gamble."

Pascal quirked a black-as-sin brow and directed a glint of amusement toward Celeste. "Is that so?"

Celeste scowled, and he grinned as if he were the recipient of some fabulous joke. "I believe we make our own luck," she said tightly, "and not by some throw of the dice."

He shrugged, his grin widening. "You may be right." He swept a hand around the room, his jacket cracking open, drawing her gaze to his tanned throat and white dress shirt that hugged the faint ripple of his abs. "Just don't go letting everyone know, hmm? Not everyone shares your obvious...passion."

Breath lodged in her throat. Oh, she felt passion all right. And never before had it burned so fever bright! "I'll keep that in mind," she managed, all too aware of his spicy male scent, his intoxicating nearness.

Lexie winked broadly at Pascal, before turning to her friend with a smirk. "Why *did* you come tonight? I'm betting it isn't for my scintillating company."

Celeste had learned to despise probing questions almost as much as she did unwanted physical contact. But she'd adapted, outmaneuvering most queries and becoming ambiguous with others. "You're right." She lifted her glass. "I come solely for the pink champagne."

As she swallowed the last of her drink, Pascal's eyes danced with mirth. One corner of his lips tilted. "I imagine you'd come for something more gratifying than that."

Lexie guffawed at the smoothly delivered double entendre, her mind evidently no longer on her friend or the roulette wheel as she raked a suggestive look over his black-suited body. "She mightn't, but I would."

Something toxic and nasty seared Celeste's belly, an emotion she didn't want to examine too closely. Pascal was a hot body, a man to satisfy her insatiable urges—nothing more. Lexie was welcome to him, *after* Celeste was done with him.

Her womb clenched with anticipation at the mere thought of Pascal's cock buried deep inside her. Then her chest constricted as another image flashed—Lexie entwined with Pascal, her abundant breasts filling his hands, her silken hair wrapped around him like a midnight cloak.

Pascal held out a crooked elbow, pointedly ignoring the other woman's come-on. "May I?"

Placing her empty glass onto a passing waiter's tray, Celeste considered him, faking indecision she certainly didn't feel.

Pascal was obviously familiar with her hands-off rule. She wasn't the infamous "ice queen" for nothing. Then again, had this man ever observed convention? Her pulse kicked into top gear. He was high-risk, dangerous. And she'd never been more tempted.

She slowly nodded and stepped toward him, repressing a shiver when she clasped the crook of his arm as though her hand belonged there. She could almost feel the sparks shooting from Lexie's narrowed stare as Pascal escorted her through the crowd of high-stakes gamblers.

There was no need to ask where they were headed. The sexual heat hung like an aura between them, conveying more than any words their destination.

She saw his nostrils flare and wondered absently if he'd scented the musky bouquet at the juncture of her thighs, caught the whiff of her arousal.

Their reflections became visible as they approached the mirrored double doors of a private elevator. They truly were light and shade, fire and ice. Together they looked...perfect.

Her upswept blonde hair shone silver-bright next to the styled blue black of Pascal's. Her slender body encased in unrelenting white was sharp contrast to his powerful frame in a sleek, dark, tailored suit.

Even in stilettos she barely reached Pascal's dark-stubbled jaw and she wished, not for the first time, that she hadn't inherited her mother's petite gene. She shook her head. It was such an inane concern in comparison to the grotesque, leathery wings sprouting from her spine.

Perhaps her deformity would have been easier to bear if she'd also inherited her gargoyle father's enhanced senses and strength. Instead, she was nothing more than a human with a deformity. Only time would tell if she'd age as a human, as her mother did, or stay immortal like her father.

Security men stepped aside from their positions on either side of the elevator doors and Pascal murmured a greeting before guiding her inside.

The doors pinged shut and they shot upward. When Pascal moved to face her, she dropped his arm with a shocked gasp, only to have him clasp her chin for an infinitesimal second and look into her eyes.

She felt oddly weak-kneed, powerless to prevent his touching her. She was aware that her pulse thundered in her ears as he said huskily, "I've watched you, wanted you, *ached* for you, from the moment I first saw you."

Chapter Two

Her eyelids drifted shut as she recalled that day, almost one month previous, as though it were just yesterday.

She'd attended a charity auction that had secured a real coup. Yves Carrington-Moore, a highly sought after but zealously secretive artist, had donated a small collection of some of the most amazing bronze sculptures she'd ever seen. She'd been unable to stop herself from bidding on a slender, life-sized female gargoyle figure. Its subtle ugliness had also conveyed a fragile beauty that was captivating and, for her, somehow tender.

With the bids around her quickly escalating, she'd raised the offer to a staggering amount. Then the unthinkable had happened, and from across the room a sexy, deep voice far surpassed her bid.

She'd searched the crowd for the man behind the voice. And her stare had clashed with eyes the color of brilliant amber. Tiger's eyes.

All sounds had faded until only they'd existed. She'd been filled to the brim with a need impossible to ignore, a burning heat yet to be ignited. Her pussy might have cramped almost painfully with lust, but panic had also soared. The self-control she'd prided herself on was slipping irrevocably from her grasp.

She'd managed to put one more offer on the sculpture. Pascal hadn't bothered, he'd clearly achieved what he wanted—her undivided attention. The moment she'd sealed the deal, she'd fled the auction. Fled from Pascal and his intense, smoldering stare. Fled from her own confused emotions.

The gargoyle sculpture in her huge loft apartment was now a constant, perverse reminder of a man she was unable to forget, no matter how hard she tried.

"Celeste."

Her eyes snapped open. Her name sounded exotic on his tongue. And so very, very possessive.

"I know you feel the same," he murmured, the ridiculously long sweep of his lashes dropping low, "despite the frigid act you try so hard to maintain."

She slipped free from his grasp, the moist heat pooling between her thighs something no bona-fide ice queen should experience. "So confident," she said. "Tell me, are the two women you left at the blackjack table happy to share?"

He quirked a brow. "They don't have a choice."

As the elevator doors slid soundlessly apart, they stayed put, caught by the ever-increasing heat thickening the air.

Her throat burned. "You fucked them both?"

He lifted a hand to her mouth, his fingertips smoothing across her lips. "Such a harsh word from such soft, pretty lips."

"Answer me." *Damn you.*

His stare turned thoughtful, never once leaving hers. "They pleasured me, just as I pleasured them." His hand dropped and he shrugged. "It's not uncommon for more than one woman at a time to warm my sheets."

His blunt honesty should have seen her turn tail and run in the opposite direction. Instead, a deep, aching restlessness burst into something deliciously hot and forbidden.

Pascal blew out a breath before tunneling a hand through his hair. "I've never leashed my desires, never had reason to pledge a woman my commitment. Just as I never gave any lover a reason to believe they were more than a passing diversion."

He cocked his head to the side and she felt as if all her thoughts were exposed as he studied her with his tiger eyes. "I'm certain you wouldn't have stepped into my private elevator, come to my penthouse suite with me, if you weren't ready and willing—"

She stood on tiptoe, leaning forward to slant her lips across his in an action that spoke so much louder than words. She sighed, savoring the fullness of his mouth, the decadent taste of spice and scotch.

With an almost soundless groan, he returned the kiss, deepened it, his skill all too apparent as his tongue skated across her lower lip before sliding inside her mouth with an ease that screamed bedroom prowess.

When his hands spanned her waist, she jerked free, gasping for breath and wishing desperately that she had nothing to hide...nothing to fear. "No," she uttered. "If we're intimate tonight, it will be under my conditions, or not at all."

Pascal's expression bore no hint of disapproval or surprise, just a fleeting curiosity. "No touching, hmm?"

Her heart fluttered like a moth beating itself against a light bulb. "Something like that." Gathering her composure, she swept past him, out of the elevator and onto a gleaming expanse of white tiles.

Motion sensors triggered a series of down-lights to illuminate the huge penthouse suite. She shivered under their glare as Pascal followed her, close behind. Even without the clack-clack of her stilettos, she wouldn't have heard his tread. He moved with the stealth of a predator. Only a fixated awareness of him allowed her to perceive the moment he released her from his sights.

She turned, watching as he strode over to a well-stocked bar. His jacket pulled taut across his broad shoulders as he bent and opened the door to a mini-fridge. Retrieving a chilled bottle of champagne, he uncorked it with deft hands and filled two glasses.

She looked away, suddenly nervous and inexplicably afraid. What had she been thinking? Pascal was a man who took control, shaped his destiny and commanded his lot in life. He was a man who, she had no doubt, yearned to touch, to feel, to caress and possess the woman in his bed.

She swallowed hard. Heaven help her, she wanted to be that woman!

With jerky steps she made her way toward a huge floor-to-ceiling window, barely seeing the velvet night with its vista of city lights spread out as far as the eye could see. She stilled and the clamoring jumble of her emotions also stilled, frozen, numb, until outwardly at least, she was no longer a quivering mass of jelly.

From close behind, too close for her peace of mind, he asked, "Are you okay?" His husky voice was like warm honey drizzled over her anesthetized nerves, bringing them back to life.

"I'm fine." She turned and snared the glass he proffered, careful not to make contact. She would *not* fall victim to a desire to be touched. She was certain she wouldn't want him to stop at just brushing against her fingers. Hell, she wanted his hands all over her, stroking and caressing.

But she'd wither and die before allowing anybody—this man in particular—to feel or see her wings. It'd shatter her spirit, having to watch his face contort with shock, his stare glaze with disgust. A man like Pascal, who'd dated and bedded the crème de la crème of beautiful women...well, she wouldn't need a psychology degree to analyze his reaction.

In truth, her self-image phobia was nothing short of trivial when compared to what she and her dad lived with every day—the ever-present danger of being captured and studied, caged like wild animals.

Quite simply, no one could ever be allowed to discover her secret.

He raised his glass and took a swallow, ever-watchful. "My god, you really don't like to be touched, do you?"

"Do you have a problem with that?" she countered, all too ready to find an excuse to leave. All too ready to find a reason to stay.

"Yes. As a matter of fact, I do." His eyes flashed. "But I'm a patient man. I can bide my time."

She didn't want to think about the implications he'd voiced. Things wouldn't be any different after tonight, no matter how much either of them might wish otherwise. "No," she whispered, throat tight. "Tonight is all we'll ever have."

Chapter Three

"That's where you're wrong," Pascal refuted, setting his glass onto an occasional table with a sharp clack before striding toward her.

Resisting the urge to backpedal, she instead lifted her drink and drained it dry. When he took away her empty glass, his fingers brushed hers, sending a scalding flood of heat through her.

"One night won't be enough," he murmured huskily, "for either of us."

Heaven help her, she didn't have the strength to voice further objection, didn't have the willpower to pretend to resist the man she wanted more than any man ever before. And when he deliberately cupped her face with gentle hands—as though dealing with the finest piece of porcelain—his mouth dropping to cover hers, she was powerless, mesmerized.

She gasped, her wings twitching uselessly beneath their restraint. He kissed her with a tender mastery that was exquisite. His tongue slid past her lips and twined with hers, sending a jolt of heat down her spine before ricocheting straight between her thighs and hardening her nipples into sharp buds.

He drew back, his amber eyes searching her face. "I'd bet my life that you're anything but an ice queen."

Anger spiked alongside desire, pushing her straight into self-protect mode. "Is that what this is all about? A bet? A quest to break down my defenses?"

His head reared back farther, his stare narrowing. She gritted her teeth. Had she hit too close to the truth?

"Some bets are best left at the gaming tables," he said. "I wish only to know the woman in my arms. Inside and out."

Goose bumps raced over her suddenly chilled skin. She could never grant him that wish. "Then you'll be sadly disappointed."

"I doubt that very much."

His throaty voice made her breasts ache and she throbbed in places only he could make better. She might be human in almost every way, but not for the first time, she had to wonder if her sexual needs weren't all gargoyle.

Of course her cold persona was a sham. But why, when she'd fucked male escorts who were the best and most learned in the sex industry, had she been left frustrated and incomplete, as if she were an unlit firecracker primed to explode? Oh, she'd enjoyed the sex, the act of joining, but after the residual effects of pleasure had dulled, she'd become an empty shell. A husk.

No longer. She knew somehow that she was on the cusp of detonation. Every fiber of her being acknowledged that tonight, Pascal would light that fuse.

"There's only one way to find out," she whispered.

A pulse jerked to life at the side of his jaw. "No small talk, no getting to know each other first?"

She guessed it wasn't often someone blindsided him. "No." Her head tilted, her eyelids sweeping half-mast as she studied his sensual lower lip, his strong jaw with its shadowed beginnings of stubble. "I'd prefer we skip the mental foreplay and cut straight to the chase."

He laughed, the rich sound warming her senses, fanning the flames of her need. His arms spread outward. "Then I'm all yours."

This time it was she who came to him, the sizzle of electricity between them palpable even before she slid her hands inside his warm jacket. She drew it over his broad shoulders, down his lean, muscled arms while all the time his gaze snared hers.

"I burn to hold you, to feel you," he said hoarsely.

Oh, I burn for that too.

"Don't...don't say anything more," she said, gulping back a sudden, insane weakness to voice consent. Instead, she forced her eyes away from his and focused on undoing each button on his shirt, baring his chest with its crisp sprinkling of dark hairs that arrowed to his navel, his flat belly.

She parted his shirt, pressing kisses to his golden skin that tasted faintly of spice and delicious, erotic male. She flicked her tongue over his hard nipples. He groaned and said throatily, "You don't play fair."

She drew back, catching his stare again as she helped him shrug out of his shirt. "Haven't you heard the expression: All's fair in love and war?"

"But when has either one ever been fair?" he rasped, his chest flaring in and out as though he'd run an exhilarating race and won, his toned torso looking every inch as though he really was an athlete.

"You tell me?" she said, crouching to undo the clasp on the waistband of his tailored pants. As the fastener parted, she took hold of his zipper and pulled it downward ever so slowly.

His breath caught. "I've never been in love," he managed to voice. "But I've seen the results. Not pretty."

"You've clearly never met my parents."

He toed off his boots. "A love match, then?"

"Yes." Soul mates.

"So you're looking for the same?"

Once, such a question would have caused her to die a little inside. Now she'd almost come to accept the fact she'd never find great love. Not in this lifetime. Not with her wings. "No." She shook her head. "No. Definitely not."

When she tugged his pants down his muscular thighs and calves, it was done with a little more force than necessary. But anger gave way to another rousing swell of desire when her eyes lined up directly with the bulge of his erection barely contained by his jocks.

Oh, mercy.

"Why not?" he asked, stepping out of one pants leg and then the other before peeling off his socks.

She swallowed past a suddenly parched throat. He was leaving her to release his cock from his underwear. She looked up. "Would you ask me that if I was a man?"

He grinned. "I wouldn't be in this position if you were, so I guess we'll never know."

"I guess not."

She leaned forward and dipped her tongue into his navel. His moan edged into a ragged gasp when she licked around its outer rim.

As the faint suggestion of salt and musky male hit her taste buds, she suddenly wanted to sample his cock, suck the head and shaft into her mouth, over her tongue and down her throat.

She straightened, realizing she too was breathing heavily. He proffered her a hand and, without thought her fingers entwined with his, allowing him to draw her beside him and into his spacious bedroom, toward his huge four-poster bed draped in a patterned spread of red and black.

Talking seemed unnecessary. He turned to her. But before his hands could tug her close and outline her waist, her back...her wings, she instructed hoarsely, "Lie down."

A smile played on his lips as he dropped his hands to his sides and moved onto the bed. He stretched out. God, she found it so sexy when a male didn't try to dominate, when he was happy to succumb, even just for a little while.

She only wished she too could be so at ease.

She swallowed yet again, her throat drying further at the sight of Pascal on the bed. Even in his underwear he was sinfully sexy, and though it was perverse to want to see his flesh while not granting him the same satisfaction in return, right then she didn't much care.

He watched her intently, his voice a rasp as he murmured, "Just for the record, I'm not averse to the idea of finding what your parents had. True love definitely has its appeal."

She smiled, perhaps a little too brightly, while inside she ached with a longing she'd genuinely started to believe was long suppressed. Her vision blurred at the edges, tears threatening to spill free.

Pascal frowned. "I didn't mean to—"

She shook her head, cutting off his apology before things became too personal. Awkward. She moved closer to the side of the bed, trailing her fingertips just above the waistband of his jocks.

His cock jerked, passion instantly reasserted by her touch. He groaned when her fingers caught hold of his jocks and slowly pulled them down, exposing the bead of pre-cum oozing from the slitted helmet of his cock, the broad shaft roped with veins. He was long and hard, a good eight inches of silky smooth cock with coarse sprigs of hair surrounding its base.

She knelt on the bed and shuffled forward. With unsteady hands she tugged his jocks free, tossing them aside and feeling decidedly wet between her thighs. "Don't move," she instructed hoarsely.

With more speed than grace, she climbed off the bed and spun away. Stepping inside his huge walk-in closet and past rows of tailored jackets and shirts, she found innumerable neckties draped over custom racks. Plucking four at random, she retraced her steps.

His fingers were interlaced behind his head in a casual pose but his thick, hard cock looked anything but relaxed. She squeezed her thighs together, demanding huskily, "Spread your legs."

He arched a brow but she detected the glint in his eyes as he drawled, "Kink, on our first date?"

"I'm sure you've participated in a spot of bondage before."

"Yes, many times. Just not with an ice queen."

As she trussed his ankles to first one post and then the other, he deliberately and shamelessly rocked his hips, flaunting the motion of the sexual act with his ever-thickening cock. Need coiled inside her belly and made her panties wetter still. She gave the last knot at his ankle an extra tug.

He wiggled a little, this time seemingly to get more comfortable. He swept a long look at her deft hands. "You're well practiced."

It wasn't a question.

As she tethered his wrists she tried not to think about the satiny skin on the underside of his arm, the slightly calloused hardness of his palms, which seemed odd for a man of his profession. Then she looked up, her eyes level with his straining erection and making her lose her train of thought about everything but sating her ever growing needs.

She jerked her head up another few degrees and focused on his face. "Do my tying skills bother you?" she asked huskily.

"Baby, it excites me." He jerked his head toward his cock. "Arouses me." His chuckle edged into a groan. "I'm about ready to come and you're not even undressed yet."

Need flared in her belly and arrowed like a homing missile straight between her thighs. Her hands trembled as she did a final check of his bonds before she turned away—fled?—on heels that sank into luxurious Berber carpet. She crossed the room in search of a light switch, finding one near a double set of closed blinds.

"Wait," he called out hoarsely.

She stilled, but didn't turn to view the man lying spread-eagle on his own bed. It was very nearly orgasmic to see this powerful man trussed up, making him vulnerable to her every whim. But right now she needed all her wits. It would gain her nothing to collapse in a drooling, panting heap beside his bound and naked body.

"Don't turn the lights out," he said. "I want to see—"

"No." Something jagged coursed through her, a painful yearning laced with a bitterness that even now, alongside so much desire, had the ability to deeply wound. "You won't see me naked."

Not ever.

A bedpost creaked. "Celeste. Look at me."

His gentle voice leached a stupid tear from one eye. She swiped it away, angry at herself, angrier at him. She didn't need his sympathy. She swung to face him.

"I only wish to see you with your hair down."

She closed her eyes. "Oh."

She always wore her hair up. It was so very long, probably too long, but with her wings so hideously ugly, the bountiful tresses were the one vanity she kept just for herself.

She dragged her eyelids apart, then took hold of the diamond-edged slide beneath her coiled hair and pulled it free. Shaking her head, she felt the weight of her hair slither just below her waist, one silver-blonde lock falling over her brow, past her chin and dipping over one of her breasts.

"Fuck me," he breathed. "You're gorgeous."

His words, his gleaming stare, caused her blood to run hot. She swallowed, then reached behind her, flicking the switch and plunging the room into darkness. "Beauty is only skin deep," she croaked, even as waves of pleasure filled her to overflowing as she stalked back to his bed.

Chapter Four

She could see little more than shapes and outlines—his bed and side tables, the en suite door and, as her eyes adjusted, his vague, shadowy silhouette. His ragged breaths were startlingly loud, as was the whispered rasp of the coverlet beneath his restless body, the chafe of his ties along the bedposts.

She shivered with need and her wings rippled in response. Damn. She was so wet for him.

The bed creaked as he shifted again and he finally murmured, "So I've been told. But is it so wrong for a man to appreciate a beautiful woman's body in all its natural glory?"

Not if that woman truly was beautiful all over, normal. "I guess it depends how confident that woman is about her body...about her lover."

Let him dwell on that!

She climbed onto the bed and back between his legs, a feeling like none other—a rush, a high—surging through her as she ran her hands over his taut, washboard belly, along his hard hips, his strong thighs. "It's been my experience that men get off not being in the driver's seat. Get off lying on their back while receiving all the attention."

When Pascal next spoke it sounded as if he bit out his words through gritted teeth. "Some might say phone sex would be as intimate—"

He inhaled sharply as she dropped low and ran her tongue along the underside of his cock. Bringing her mouth to the head, she tasted the bead of pre-cum and licked him dry, enjoying its salty aftertaste that was all male and somehow tantalizingly immoral. "You were saying?"

"You. Are. Killing. Me."

She grinned. It was exhilarating, a turn-on, knowing she had Pascal at her mercy like this, his straining cock and heavy balls exposed to the night air and her touch.

She pushed off the bed and tugged the bodice of her dress down, over her bound breasts and wings before allowing it to drop onto the floor. Pascal shifted again, the bedcover rustling at his impatience, and she couldn't help but smile as she unhooked her corset and let it slip to the floor.

"Damn, I wish I could see you," he said.

She stiffened, her smile freezing. *Oh, Pascal. Be careful what you wish for.*

Years of self-discipline stilled her wings, withstood the reflexive urge to stretch them, flap out the kinks and swipe one leathery wingtip along Pascal's throat, down his belly and along his rigid cock.

She stepped out of her panties and took a moment to enjoy the caress of air on her bared pussy, on each bony protrusion along the ribs of her unbound wings and her peaked nipples. It was both exhilarating and disturbing to stand naked before a lover with only the velvet kiss of night to hide her deformity.

Climbing back onto the bed, she moved over him until the underside of her thighs glanced against his belly, her pussy aligned to his navel. She felt him tense, awaiting full contact. It'd take little effort to move back against his cock until it jutted vertically, before impaling herself on him.

Instead, she leaned down, pressing kisses along his throat and up to his earlobe. He groaned as she moved to cover his mouth with hers. Her pussy lips slid shamelessly across his skin and she gasped into his mouth when her clit scraped along the puckered halo of his navel.

His head reared back. His body jerked, straining for hers. "Baby, this is torture," he growled. "I want to be inside you. I want you to ride me, fuck me."

Her core spasmed at his husky words, at the instinctive rhythm of his body as he writhed beneath her, searching for relief...at the thought of her juices on his skin. Tingling warmth became a quivering heat wave and she froze, shocked by the realization a climax had been about to fling her to its starry heights and beyond.

She sucked in a breath. Giving his ear a nip she whispered hoarsely, "We'll fuck when I'm ready." Climax or not, this was her night, on her terms. And god help her for being selfish, she wasn't about to let Pascal forget.

"Then be warned. I'm a heartbeat away from orgasm," he muttered thickly.

In the utter darkness, she clamped a hand over his cock and raised herself high, positioning the slit of her pussy over his engorged length. "Not without me." In the next breath she dropped onto him all the way, stretching her inner walls to capacity, filling herself with his dimensions.

He hissed as she mewled with a pleasure that bordered on pain. Slumping full-length along him, she waited until her muscles adjusted and accepted him fully. She wiggled a little, testing for pain, and he groaned, the bedposts rattling an encore as he attempted to reach out.

Her wings shivered but remained tucked in a neat compression of folds along her spine. Even almost delirious with need there was no chance in hell she'd give him reason to suspect she wasn't quite human. She sat up, straddling him and running outspread hands along the warmth of his chest, the light sprinkle of his hairs rasping under her palms.

Then lifting her hips until Pascal's cock was almost free, she plunged all the way back down.

He groaned. "Oh, baby. Yeah..."

As she rode him in an ever-increasing rhythm that had her panting and gasping, the bedsprings creaking protest as his hips thrust upward to meet her tempo, she distantly wished she could watch his eyes glaze, see his sexy mouth part in utter ecstasy before he roared her name, spilling his seed deep inside her.

Then she forgot what she'd been thinking as her body abruptly convulsed, each spasm lighting her up from within and exploding in ever-increasing waves of pleasure that ricocheted all the way to her toes.

Seconds—minutes?—later, she collapsed onto his chest with her hair spilling around them, totally drained of energy and yet sexually replete in every way.

No longer was she an empty shell. She'd never felt so satisfied, so feminine, so complete. It was as though Pascal was the missing piece she'd unconsciously sought out. And now there was a part of her that'd pine even more come their separation.

Her parents were soul mates, she was certain of it...but her and Pascal? The very idea was almost too bizarre to contemplate. And yet, it played with her mind, teased her heart with its implications until she knew she couldn't stay even one moment longer.

Oh, it'd be only too easy to stay wrapped around him, enjoying the physical intimacy that on some deeper level had become almost poignant. But she couldn't. Every passing second meant a separation that would be all the harder to endure.

She pushed upright, disengaging from his already hardening cock before she had a chance to change her mind. He didn't voice an objection, but she heard his sharp intake of breath, sensed his conflict as he lay there, waiting for her next move.

With a sigh, she retrieved her corset and hooked it together at the front.

Her panties were elusive so she left them and dragged her dress over her head before flicking on the light switch.

Desire leapt to life in her belly, her core, at Pascal's dilemma. His cock was already thick and erect, more than capable of bringing her pleasure...and to orgasm once more. But she'd have to be content with just one sexual act—more and intimacy might become too familiar, too easily ceded, with mistakes too easily made.

Ignoring a hundred fantasies springing to mind, she untied his ankles first and then freed his arms. He stretched, completely unashamed, and she could barely tear her eyes away from the flex and shift of his lean washboard abs, his cock jutting long, hard and ever ready from its dark nest of curls.

Right then she wanted nothing more than to slip into his arms and feel them settle around her. Wanted nothing more than to savor his mouth, his hands on her skin as they explored each other the way lovers were meant to.

Her chest felt tight as she leaned down, unable to resist pressing a chaste peck goodbye on his cheek. He immediately turned and captured her mouth with his, deepening the kiss—owning it—before she wrenched away.

"You're the one not playing fair," she gasped.

"If I have to fight dirty to keep you, I will." He snared her hand, his fingers moving to stroke the galloping pulse at her wrist. "Don't go."

Chapter Five

She almost surrendered. Instead she gulped back a little mewl of need and said, "I can't stay."

His hand slipped up her arm in a caress, not quite releasing her. "Why?"

Her wings unfurled a little beneath the restriction of her corset and this time she was helpless to stop them. She pulled free of his grasp. "I don't want a relationship."

Really? a little voice asked inside her head.

He shrugged. "So you want your freedom. I can deal with that." He smirked but she saw the serious edge lurking behind his stare. "I get it, really. You don't like to be...tied down."

Celeste couldn't help but smile at his implication, then felt a frown overlay the spark of joy as it dawned on her that she shouldn't be there, exchanging small talk with this primal, dangerous man. Shouldn't be listening to his slumberous voice with its undercurrents of seriousness. Except, being with him was addictive and intoxicating even as it was scary, like walking on a tightrope with sharp-edged diamonds beckoning far below.

"I guess you're right," she conceded lamely. "I don't like to be tied down." Literally. She'd had enough of that with having to batten down her wings. Giving another, much weaker smile, she turned, her scattered wits operating just enough to be able to walk away.

"Celeste."

She stilled, then like a marionette with no self-control, she pivoted to face him. Her heart lurched. He looked so damn fine—edible, with his sexy, rumpled hair, his seductive lips, which she suddenly imagined bringing her to orgasm in the best possible way.

Liquid heat gathered at the juncture of her thighs, reminding her of her lack of underwear.

"At the very least allow me to take you out to dinner."

"I'm not sure that's such a good idea." And yet, she was tempted. So very, very tempted.

He stood and, in just a couple of strides, was right before her. She should have felt dwarfed without her shoes. Only, he made her feel as if she were the most important person in the world as he reached out and trailed a thumb along one side of her jaw.

Her skin burned beneath his touch and she realized he was taking yet another liberty. She may have joined with Pascal in the most intimate way possible but she'd disabled his ability to touch and caress for good reason. And though she'd taken hold of his arm as he'd escorted her, it'd been she who'd touched him.

She jerked back, forcing her gaze to his chin level and above.

He quirked a dark brow. "It's just dinner."

Was he right? Had she overanalyzed things? Would a meal in a casino restaurant with people all around them really hurt? She cleared her suddenly thick throat. "I don't date."

"Okay. So it's not a date. Just two people enjoying each other's company."

Then why did she get the sudden impression she'd be the dessert? And why did that fill her with a need so sudden and strong she felt faint?

His expression was closed but his eyes glittered knowingly, as if he were aware of her dilemma, and she wondered frantically if she'd break her own cardinal rule by sleeping with a man more than once. Even as the thought flitted through her mind, she found herself shrugging and saying, "Sure. Why not."

She spotted her lacy panties, bent and scooped them up. They were sopping wet. She frowned and heard wry amusement in Pascal's voice as he challenged softly, "You could always go without your underwear."

She twisted to face him. "You think an ice queen wouldn't have the nerve?"

His yellow eyes flared into a deep amber-orange color. "I think the real question is—*are* you an ice queen?"

Her fingers clenched for a moment, then unlocked. The minuscule piece of lace dropped noiselessly to the floor.

Pascal nodded, not bothering to conceal the triumph burning in his stare. He gestured toward her abandoned panties. "I'll have room service dry clean these for you."

"Thank you," she managed, mouth dry as she watched him swing around and stride toward his walk-in closet. There was some kind of lettering etched into the length of his spine. Add his taut buttocks, muscled thighs and broad shoulders, and he was almost too perfect to be true.

Not everyone has to hide a secret.

She blew out a breath. Perhaps there weren't many who needed to hide something on the outside. But she'd bet her considerable fortune almost everyone had something to hide on the inside. Pascal, she was certain, was one of them.

She was refastening her hair into its thick coil behind her nape when he reappeared a few minutes later, dressed a little more informally in a pair of dark slacks and a crimson dress shirt that dramatically emphasized his dark coloring.

Celeste shunted between excitement and numb panic, which only increased as Pascal's brooding stare landed on her time and again while they rode the elevator to the ground floor.

Within the building, a handful of twenty-four-hour restaurants catered to the gambling crowd. Pascal chose one that appeared discreet and upscale. The plush dining area was sprinkled with late-night diners but Celeste scarcely noticed as Pascal caught her hand in his and led her between the labyrinth of damask-covered tables, his powerful frame a strong silhouette beneath the glittering chandeliers.

They found a booth in an alcove that afforded them a modicum of privacy. She was glad for their solitude. She ached suddenly for Pascal to touch her between her thighs, to open her wide and expose her pink flesh, her throbbing clit, to his stare.

He waited for her to be seated before he slid into the bench seat opposite. He lounged back, outwardly relaxed and yet clearly only too aware of her arousal. Behind the flame of a single candle, his gaze glinted sexual heat while she squirmed, seeking respite from the needs clamoring within.

A drinks waitress hurried over, and Celeste requested a glass of champagne. She'd broken every other of her self-enforced rules since being with Pascal, what was one more? She rarely drank, particularly in the company of a man who made her toes curl with just a look. Too much alcohol and it was all too feasible she'd relax and let her guard down, do something she'd regret later, like allowing his hand to drift along her spine...

She chewed her bottom lip, mulling over the reasons why she acted so out of character around Pascal. Did his dangerous side attract the simmering, passionate nature she'd had to hide so long from the world? Was there more between them than simple lust and chemistry? Were they kindred spirits drawn to each other?

"Make that a bottle," Pascal ordered with an amused smile. "I believe I have a dozen or more crates of vintage stock in storage."

The pretty waitress's blue eyes widened, recognition dawning. "Oh, of course, sir." She blushed, fumbling at a tendril of dark hair that had escaped its chignon. "I'll get that for you right away."

"Do you always have that effect on women?" Celeste queried as the waitress hurried away. She batted her eyelashes as though she too was afflicted with the I-adore-you-Pascal syndrome.

Damned if she wasn't.

He grinned with shameless amusement. "Nearly always." He adjusted his collar. "Is it getting hot in here, or is it just me?"

She swallowed, shifting again as he slowly unbuttoned the top two buttons of his shirt. She absently noted he wasn't wearing a tie before seconds later she heard one of his shoes thump onto the floor.

"What are you doing?" she squeaked, aware he'd also slipped off his sock.

"Getting comfortable."

When she felt his bare foot skimming between her thighs, a flash of heat, pure and unadulterated, seared her pussy. She was a passionate woman by nature—gargoyle or human?—and pretending otherwise by leading a double life as an ice queen at times half killed her.

Her head fell back and with the softest sigh she closed her eyes, opening herself to his questing touch.

"That's it," he murmured throatily, his voice having her instantly imagine sex and sun and cold whipped cream on her hot, waxed pussy. His foot moved upward. "Let yourself go, enjoy the moment, the pleasure."

When his toes nudged her outer lips apart before deftly massaging her aching clit, she sucked in a breath, torn between letting him call the shots and hauling back a control that was spiraling quickly out of control.

"One bottle of champagne, Sir, Madam."

Pascal stilled his ministrations and Celeste cracked open an eye, way beyond pretending normalcy. Either the waitress was too well trained to reveal awareness as she uncorked the bottle, or didn't need a vivid imagination to realize just how easily one would succumb to Pascal's expertise.

Her mind whirred. Or had Pascal done this before, with other women in this very same booth?

After pouring them each a glass, the waitress said with a wry smile, "Enjoy the rest of your night."

Pascal grinned at Celeste like a wolf tormenting a cornered hare, prompting her to hiss, "How could you?"

"Could I what?"

"Sit there so innocently while—" Her words ended on a strangled gasp as his big toe circled her clit a little harder, a little faster. Her head fell back, her thighs opening wider still. "You really are a bad, bad boy," she said weakly, clutching at the tabletop as if her life depended on it.

"For you, I could be good," he rasped.

Good...as in faithful? Permanent? A lover?

Her heart fluttered, desperate, needy. Despite the rebuttal forming on her lips, despite the list of reasons on tap in her head, nothing formed...nothing coherent, anyway. There was little she could do but give in to the moment and enjoy the ride.

"Oh..." She gritted her teeth, the bench seat digging into her scalp as her head fell back and she came apart, electric heat sizzling through her most intimate nerve endings. Again and again.

She swallowed back another moan as his toe worked her clit again, pushing her toward a second climax. Her lids flicked open, her head too heavy somehow as she watched him through a dream-like haze. At his blatantly possessive smile her vision cleared.

She jerked back. When he withdrew his foot she slammed her legs shut, reality returning with a rush. No matter how sexually compatible, how physically connected, they would never be a couple. There would never be an "us".

She chewed her bottom lip as she gathered her battle-wearied defenses. She'd broken all her rules with Pascal, and he probably knew it. Damn it! She should never have agreed to this dinner, never have given in to a moment of weakness.

The murmur of other late-night diners, interspersed by the clatter of cutlery and the hurried tread of wait-staff, intruded on her sex-fogged mind. Her face flooded with heat but she didn't peer around to determine if anyone had been witness to her depravity—though curiously, the very thought rekindled a spark of lust, a tingling need that had her imagination running riot.

She took a deep, fortifying breath and he cocked his head, his brooding stare searching her face as he asked, "Are you okay?"

She clutched her glass of champagne and gulped some down, easing her parched throat. "Fine," she croaked, "just another day in the life of Celeste Diamond."

A waiter appeared by their table. "Sir. Madam. May I take your orders?"

Pascal flicked the menu open, which Celeste felt sure he already knew by rote. "Hmm. Perhaps I'll let my...date decide." His stare shifted back to her, and her heart immediately tripped double speed as he asked huskily, "Celeste, anything tempt you?"

She squirmed at his deliberate provocation, imagining him discarding the menu and sampling her. When his stare flashed red heat, she swallowed a groan, picturing her thighs spread apart for Pascal's visual enjoyment and him leaning in for a taste, licking and sucking her pink, quivering flesh...

"Madame?" prompted the waiter tactfully.

She cleared her throat. "Ah." She looked at Pascal and said faintly, "Surprise me."

He nodded, his golden eyes darkening and not leaving hers. "Okay. I think the home-style rib-eye steak, medium rare. He dragged his gaze from hers and said to the bemused man waiting for their order, "To share."

Clarifying their order, the waiter turned to leave, only to pause as Celeste blurted, "Wait." She smiled a challenge at Pascal before turning to the waiter. "Make the steak well done."

The waiter glanced over at Pascal, who shrugged and said easily, "Whatever the lady wants."

Alone once more, Pascal refilled her glass and then his own. "You know, you should never feel the need to establish your freedom, not for my benefit. I like your strong will, your independence." He put the empty bottle back onto the table with a firm clack. "And I'd never try to take that away from you."

Even if she had the words to express the profoundness of her relief, she couldn't have squeezed them past the sudden tightness of her throat. Instead she nodded mutely, abstractedly rubbing a finger over the condensation on her glass.

He took a sip of his champagne then deftly changed the subject. "There's something I'd like to show you after dinner."

She was aware it wasn't anything sexual—not yet—still, she immediately felt uncomfortable, restless, sensing somehow that whatever he wanted to show her would be personal. "I really need to get home."

His brow furrowed momentarily. "You have something...*someone*, to go home to?"

"No, I don't." She glared, aware of her see-sawing emotions. "Is it so wrong for me to want to go home alone, to an empty house?"

He placed his half-empty flute back on the table. "Not at all. Not if it's what you really want."

Her chest hurt, the pain spreading out like the coldest caress. All she'd ever really wanted was a husband, children, a family for her to love and to love her in return. She'd more than wanted it, she'd pined for it until it'd become a familiar deep ache that had settled over her heart like an icy fist.

It was human nature to want what one couldn't have. Perhaps that's why she craved the adoration her parents rarely shared.

A shadow fell over the table from behind her, distracting her from her thoughts. She twisted in her seat, looking up with a start.

A short, barrel-chested man peered down at them through mean, narrowed eyes.

"What is it, Lewie?" drawled Pascal, his voice lazily amused.

The other man ignored Pascal to squint at Celeste. "Your father wants to see you." His gravelly tone implied *now*.

Pascal eyed Lewie with languid indolence. "Is that so?"

She turned away from the repulsive man to focus on Pascal. The contrast was vivid—a sleek and powerful panther in its prime, facing off a spitting, flea-bitten tomcat. "It sounds like your surprise might have to wait."

Pascal's lip curled Lewie's way. "Tell Celeste's father she'll see him when she's ready. If it's urgent he knows where she is."

Lewie's arms folded. "It wasn't a request."

"Pascal—" She caught herself for a moment. His name sounded way too personal and intimate on her lips. "It's okay, really."

Lewie's mean gaze settled on her. A shiver of fear slid like an eel through her blood but she refused to shrink away as she turned and held his gaze. She raised her chin, eyes still locked with Lewie's as she said to Pascal, "On second thought, my dad can wait. I'd love to see the surprise you wanted to show me."

The man's thick, rubbery lower lip twisted into a sneer. "Bad move, sweetheart."

Pascal shot to his feet. With the speed of a cobra strike, his hand curled around Lewie's thick neck, forcing him to meet his gaze. "This lady is *not* your sweetheart. Comprehend?"

Chapter Six

Celeste felt her gaze widen, her heart wildly thumping between fright and jittery excitement. Lewie might have a bulldog body and meat-cleaver hands but she sensed Pascal's dominance—a hidden, steely strength that would more than match the other man's obvious brawn.

"Whatever you say, Sir." Though his mouth curled with defiance, Lewie's eyes were shadowed with fear.

Pascal released him as though he'd just handled poison. "Get out of here before I have you thrown out," he said with a quietness that held steel.

Celeste blew out a shaky breath the moment the apparent henchman lumbered out the restaurant doors, carrying away with him an aura of defiance and barely concealed ill will.

"I'm sorry you had to see that." Pascal's eyes softened, flashing concern. "Unfortunately my father doesn't gel with the idea of his only son parting ways with the mobster flock."

"So what's Lewie's deal, then?"

He sighed heavily. "It's a long, rather boring story."

"We have all night, apparently."

The meal arrived just then, steak basted in creamy sauce, surrounded by beer-battered fries and a handful of salad greens. The plate was placed in the middle of the table. He shrugged and said, "True. But...if I have to give up a secret, then so do you."

The very idea pushed aside the threat of Lewie as she swallowed back a sudden attack of nerves. But as Pascal sliced off a chunk of steak she said evenly, "Fair enough."

He proffered her the juicy morsel, skewered onto the prongs of his fork, his gaze holding hers as she leaned forward to accept it. Even cooked just before the point of charcoal, the meat dissolved in her mouth, bursting with a flavor that hinted at garlic and peppercorns.

"Good, isn't it," he murmured.

She nodded and closed her eyes for a moment, savoring the taste. When her lashes fluttered open, he was watching her as though she was the only thing that mattered. She swallowed. Why did eating with Pascal bring new meaning to intimacy?

"It's kind of nice to watch a woman who enjoys her food," he said huskily.

She managed an offhand shrug. "I've never had to diet." Gargoyle genetics? She picked up a beer-battered fry, waving it in the air as she said, "So tell me about this, ah, long story."

"Ah yes. The boring tale."

"I bet it's not."

He grinned. "Perhaps you're just nosy."

"Definitely."

His grin deepened but he relented and said, "Let's just say Lewie was a street kid in deep trouble when he was taken into the fold by my father."

"Now I'm really intrigued."

He cut another piece of steak. "All this happened long before I was part of the equation."

"So effectively you usurped your father's affections from him?"

"In a word—yes." He looked thoughtful as he added, "Though it's no secret my father wishes I was cast in the same mold as Lewie."

"That you're not the ideal son probably makes Lewie resent you all the more."

He chuckled. "You'd make a great counselor. But yes, I guess it does. Lewie dances to my father's tune to get a cursory pat on the back. I block my ears to my father's demands and still get a whole lot more affection."

"That's to be expected though. You're his son."

He made some inaudible sound close to a snort as she nibbled the fry. He cut another piece of steak and offered it to her. They ate in a silence that was comfortable even with the ever-present awareness between them. And it seemed all too soon when there was nothing left on the plate.

Dabbing her mouth with a napkin, she said, "I'm glad you talked me into this. It was most enjoyable." In more ways than one.

"It certainly was." His smile was wolf-like again when he leaned forward, holding a piece of the napkin and wiping one corner of her lip. "You missed a spot," he murmured huskily.

She cleared her throat, striving for control even as her skin rippled with sensation at his touch. "So, what now?"

He relaxed against the seat, yet she was starkly aware that he was anything but relaxed. Arousal pulsated from him—from her—until the air all but crackled with its energy.

"Can your surprise wait a bit longer?" she asked, hungry for him just one more time and willing suddenly to take one more risk with this man, one more sexual encounter. And damn the consequences.

His eyes glinted. Her heart beat fiercely. Then they stood as one, in unspoken acceptance of what was to come.

Foreign cravings, too starkly emotional for her peace of mind, almost overwhelmed her as they took the elevator to his penthouse suite. She wanted so badly to tuck herself close to his side, to press her body against his hard frame while enveloped in his embrace. It was a want—no, a need—so great, it was all she could do not to cave in.

It seemed a long ride skyward before a ping announced their arrival and the twin doors rolled apart. "Déjà vu," Pascal murmured huskily, waiting for her to step out of the elevator before he followed.

She turned to him then, stiff with sudden anxiety and all too familiar insecurities. He'd allowed her to tie him up once, he wouldn't allow it twice. Of this she felt suddenly, irrevocably certain.

Perhaps if she had surrendered to his touch, had allowed his arms to twine around her, she'd have been too caught up in the moment to care about her ugliness. "Pascal, I'm...I'm not so sure this is such a good idea now," she whispered, barely aware of her hand fluttering by her side.

Chapter Seven

Pascal reined back arousal at the sight of Celeste's chalk-white face, her beautiful jade eyes huge and fearful. Bloody hell! What did she take him for—some brute about to force her to his will? And as much as he ached to change her mind, he'd never once had to coerce a woman into his bed and he wasn't about to start now.

"You're probably right." He dropped his gaze to hide the heat of his stare. He mightn't be able to wilt his erection but he could at least deflect the burning in his eyes.

"What?" she whispered, clearly confused by his easy acceptance.

"Come," he said in answer, holding out his hand.

She lifted her hand and slowly placed it in his and for the second time that night he felt like a kid entrusted with his first adult secret. Did she recognize this leap of faith? And did she have any idea just how very precious it was that she'd chosen him to trust?

It was common knowledge that she hated physical contact. She always had. He should know. He'd been fascinated—no, obsessed—by gargoyles even before his father's henchmen had claimed seeing such a creature when they'd interrogated a criminal lawyer who had turned on the mob.

That had been twenty-five years ago and though Pascal had not acted on his interest for some years—he'd been just seven years old then—his intrigue had been sparked and had grown fiercely over the years until it'd become an obsession.

Eight years ago when Celeste had been seventeen and he'd been twenty-four, he'd finally hired a top investigator who had managed to uncover a suspected gargoyle—Celeste's father, Cray. But from the moment Pascal had seen Cray's beautiful family together, it'd been the daughter who'd snagged and held his interest from then on in. The PI had been pole-axed when Pascal asked him to turn his investigations to Cray's daughter.

He hadn't given a damn. At seventeen Celeste had been incredibly beautiful and elusive. At twenty-five she was even more so.

His hand swallowed hers and under his rough palm her hand was soft and smooth, her fingers entwined with his seemingly a perfect fit. He led her through a room with open cupboards filled with his tools of trade and a large table covered in plastic, breathing in the familiar earth and metal scents before he pushed open a far door and ushered her through.

They climbed a round of concrete steps that opened out onto a huge expanse of open, flat roof. Solar lights cast a dim light over the hundreds of large pots brimming with trees, shrubs and other greenery, turning stark concrete into an inviting, lush jungle.

Illuminated pathways stretched before them, one leading to a bench seat, another to an enclosed building shrouded in shadow. Pascal steered her toward the door of the building.

She nodded in the direction of the bench seat, a note of grievance edging her voice as she said, "I thought we'd sit over there."

He grinned. "Perhaps another time?"

*

Celeste stepped back, dropping his hand. Another time? A date? An abrupt dart of pleasure was as quickly followed by a hard, inner shake of her head. No, this night was all they had, all she'd allow. It would be totally reckless—insane, to wish for more.

All introspection fled when Pascal opened the door and flicked on the light switch. She gasped, her stare jerking from side-to-side. Gargoyle statues filled the atrium-like room. Some were life-size and others no bigger than an adult hand. Naked, clothed, male and female, each one was exquisitely beautiful.

Pascal stayed in the doorway as she drifted forward, touching and caressing the flowing lines, the perfect symmetry of each one she passed. She knew without asking who had created these bronzes. Yves Carrington-Moore, the one and same artist who'd created the bronze she'd bought at the charity auction where she'd met Pascal for the first time.

She whistled under her breath. These babies were worth a small fortune—probably a large one—and yet Pascal kept them all in this flimsy building, ripe for the picking. No, not ripe for the picking. Hiding these from the world on top of a casino boasting top-notch, high-tech security was probably safer than any vault.

So simple and yet so brilliant.

"Never in a million years would I have guessed you'd show me...this," she whispered, totally awed.

His tread was only just discernable behind her as he closed the distance between them and said huskily, "Art is my passion—my life."

She pivoted to face him, in that moment knowing exactly what he implied, knowing exactly who he was—even before reading the truth in his eyes. "You're the artist," she breathed out.

"Yes." He shrugged lazily, but there was a challenge deep in his stare. "I'm Yves Carrington-Moore, famous artist. I'm also Pascal Daniels, infamous womanizer and mobster son."

Her chest felt oddly tight as she whispered, "So who am I with now?"

"Does it matter? Pascal—Yves, I'll still want you more than life itself."

From anyone else it would have sounded corny, stupid even. But, oh Lord, she knew exactly how he felt. She was drawn to him, mesmerized by him. If she'd been one hundred percent human and wingless, she couldn't have been more joyous. "So you bid for your own piece of work to...to get my attention?"

"Yes." His eyes gleamed with something indefinable. "It worked, didn't it?" In answer she went on tiptoe and kissed him gently, tentatively, sighing at the little shocks of pleasure tingling along her lips. She pulled back, searching his stare. "You wanted me even then?" she asked.

He nodded. "I wanted you from the very first. I knew you were special."

To anyone else that would have been a compliment. For her "special" was no tribute. She wasn't human. Not completely. She never would be.

He grinned a little cheekily. "I'm guessing you like Yves as much as Pascal, hmm?"

"Are you saying I have to choose?" she asked weakly.

"Of course not." His eyes flared and then hardened fractionally. "I'm just relieved you're not mad I kept my...identity secret."

A sliver of unease chilled her blood. "Oh." His words hadn't been directed at her. He couldn't know! *Shit. Shit*! Could he? She raised her chin and managed coolly, "Who you were never concerned me. I never expected more than a few hours of pleasure together."

"And now?"

A change of subject was long overdue. She looked away and focused on the rows of statues, some of which gurgled water from their mouths and into bowls either held in the crook of their arms or set between their feet. "I can't believe you have so many of these...creatures," she said faintly, barely holding down her ever-growing anxiety.

"What can I say, they fascinate me."

Her stomach cramped and she pivoted back to him, only distantly aware her eyes were wet. Her voice cracked. "The same way I fascinate you?"

"Yes," he said gently. And his eyes, his brilliant, beautiful topaz eyes, told her exactly what her mind screamed couldn't be true.

He knew!

Chapter Eight

Celeste pressed a hand to her mouth, stumbling back. He reached for her and as she recoiled, his lips pulled into a tight line. She couldn't worry about his feelings right now, not when every iced-over sensibility was going into meltdown.

She stared at him, her eyes growing wide as the stark truth crashed through her mind like a train wreck she'd somehow known was about to happen—if she hadn't ignored all the warning signs. "You knew all along, didn't you?"

When her words came out hard and flat, his brow furrowed. "I've had my suspicions."

Dark anger, like bile, rose up inside. She'd spent almost a lifetime hiding her ugly wings, her true self. For what?

She lashed out, struck him across the face with an open palm. An audible crack reverberated around them—small satisfaction for the long-repressed emotions now unleashed inside her. "Bastard!"

The lines on his brow deepened into a scowl. His eyes flashed, all hot, brooding male. "Yes, I am."

Her jaw ached as she gritted her teeth. Yet even in her haze of fury she sensed the simmering waves of intensity emanating from him had little to do with her act of violence. There was something she couldn't put her finger on, something not quite right, if only dark emotion wasn't choking her mind.

"But it matters little," he added in a growl. "I want you Celeste, regardless of who you are—who I am. I hunger for you; I know you hunger for me. One night isn't going to be enough. Hell, we both knew it was never going to be enough."

Anger died a quick death and she had a sudden insane desire to laugh, to stamp her feet like a petulant child. Instead she swallowed past an ever-thickening lump in her throat while her eyes filled with scalding tears. "You don't understand."

"Don't I?" he asked, curving a hand beneath her jaw. His lightly calloused palm was tender and gentle, in direct contrast to the red imprint of her hand on his cheek. "I know about your father, about his gift." At her shocked intake of her breath he added softly, "About the gift he passed onto you."

It's no gift.

She felt the tears abruptly overflow, pouring down her face unchecked. "You're mistaken," she whispered, but she was all too aware he wasn't one bit deceived.

He couldn't possibly know everything, could he? She'd been so careful. Even her mum and dad—Loretta and Cray—had secluded themselves at their bush cabin high in the mountains, giving no one the chance to speculate and gossip about her mother's beautiful, but maturing appearance, her father's still youthful good looks.

"You know very well I'm not," he said quietly.

Oh, god. Her belly twisted as her mind tossed thoughts about like a toy boat in a churning sea. "Who else knows about my father?" Her voice rose. "About me?"

"Aside from myself, a skeptical investigator and the fading, vague memories of three of my father's lackeys the night they saw Cray. Not a soul."

"Then—" She sucked in a breath. "What is it you want from me?" Really want?

"Surely you know?"

She swept an arm out, indicating the inanimate statues as she choked out, "I've just discovered your obsession with these. I'd be pretty naïve not to wonder about your attraction to me."

He nodded in agreement. "Yes. And I'd be lying if I said I haven't long been fascinated by the possibility of other real-life gargoyles."

Other real life gargoyles? For one heart-stopping, delirious second, she truly believed he knew of other gargoyles. Then her pulses slowed, common sense rearing its head. Clearly—somehow—he'd learned of her father's gargoyle curse before discovering a small part of the genetic affliction had been passed onto her.

His amber eyes so very shrewd, yet gentle, he added, "But deep down you wonder about that possibility too, don't you? Wonder about the existence of other gargoyles." He brushed a stray lock of her long hair behind an ear. "Either way, it doesn't matter to me. Gargoyle...or not...I want you."

She swiped her tears dry with the back of her hand. "You say that now." Lifting her chin, she stepped back. "But you'll soon change your mind."

"I won't."

She tugged her dress down her bound torso and past her thighs, stepping out of it before dropping it aside. "Wait and see," she whispered.

"You don't need to—"

"Yes. I do."

A light filled his eyes and turned them golden, his stare all but glowing as she stilled before him. A light breeze ruffled some loosened strands of her hair, and then skimmed over her bare buttocks, her thighs and pussy.

She absently wondered how she must look, nude now except for her upper torso, encased in its corset. "Did you know I come with my own set of permanent wings?"

She held his unwavering stare and unhooked the corset. Pascal uttered not a word, registering no surprise as he stayed motionless, apparently spellbound, while he watched the corset slip to the floor.

Her breasts, lush for her petite size, swelled and hardened in the sexually heated air, her nipples tightening into buds. And when she unfurled her wings to their incredible eight-foot span, his eyes widened—not in horror—but in stark admiration.

It's the artist in him, an inner voice cautioned. He had an unhealthy obsession with gargoyles, no more, no less. Still, when she stretched her wings out and fanned them lightly, his awed reaction had her heart stuttering erratically with joy, her womb twisting with need.

"I can't imagine a woman more beautiful," he rasped thickly. His eyes dropped to her heavy, aching breasts, then lower, to her pussy with its thin strip of flaxen hair.

"Then show me...please," she whispered, her mind holding onto doubts even as her body thrummed with the touch of his hot stare.

In one stride he closed in. His mouth covered hers like warm, silken wax, his lips molding to hers, his tongue sliding inside her mouth, tasting her, turning her to flame until only when they needed to breathe did they pull apart, their gazes locked together.

His eyes blazed with molten need. "I want you."

She smiled. "I want you too." It was only her heart that gave a little pang of self-doubt, refusing to surrender completely.

Did he want her as a woman or as a gargoyle?

And then, in a silence emphasized by the air thickening into a molasses of need between them, she heard a stampede of approaching footsteps coming up the stairs and toward the storage building.

Pascal's eyes flashed. "What the hell...?"

She backed away, gasping alarm when a dozen or more men burst through the atrium door with Lewie and an older man—Pascal's dad?—in the lead. Stealth clearly not a priority, they came to a stunned standstill just twenty meters away.

The older man smiled a lascivious, twisted smirk before he drawled, "Good work, Son."

Pascal let loose a snarled expletive and then turned to her and uttered, "It's not what you think."

Isn't it?

Celeste swallowed hard, her gut churning and leaving behind a sickening, bitter residue. Tears sprung to her eyes. What a stupid fool she was for placing her trust—a piece of her heart—in this man's hands. She'd fallen right into Pascal's trap. Set up: game, set and match.

With the burn of Pascal's stare staying on her, she used her hateful wings to encircle her torso, concealing her nudity from him and from the men now openly staring her, their expressions caught between lust and revulsion.

She sucked in an agonized, disbelieving breath, refusing to look at Pascal as she numbly scooped up her dress and corset. She couldn't speak. What could she say when it felt as though her soul was being torn in two?

When she backed away another couple of steps, Pascal jerked his head to where a door beckoned at the end of the atrium. "It's unlocked." But as she paused, indecisive, he demanded hoarsely, "Go!"

She didn't need to be told twice. Tucking her wings close to her spine for maximum agility and speed, she spun around and sprinted to the door. Thrusting it open, she raced toward the edge of the casino building. She choked back a sob, not once looking behind to see if Pascal followed. It was over between them. She would never be so stupid again. Ever.

"Stop, or we'll shoot!"

She recognized Lewie's voice. Stop? Hell, no. No bullets were fired when her stride lengthened. But she knew none would be. Keeping her alive made her much more valuable. Scientists could study her DNA, take countless x-rays, test the strength and mobility of her wings whilst jabbing needles into her to dope her up or draw out her blood.

Without slowing, she kicked off from the ledge into a dive. Hugging her clothing to her torso, she snapped open her wings. Air immediately pushed her upward, halting her freefall. Dipping a wing, she soared into air currents that took her between the concealment of two office buildings, where a thinning updraft saw her rapidly descend.

Her heart thudded. Anxiety clawed at her insides, competing with an aching sadness she couldn't think upon right then.

She landed in a small but shadowy, tree-filled park just four blocks from her apartment. Though the dewy grass was cold underfoot, sweat prickled her skin. She hurriedly rewrapped her torso, dragging the dress over her head as she raced across the park lawn sprinkled with crackling leaves and litter, the sharp scent of eucalyptus filling her lungs.

Thankful for the lack of people and traffic at this predawn hour of the morning, she pounded barefoot across the narrow asphalt road lit by flickering streetlamps and then high-tailed it past closed cafes, convenience stores and dimly lit apartment buildings.

Gasping for breath, she finally stumbled into her own building—a converted, high-ceilinged double storey warehouse with the security of three apartments at ground level and her spacious, loft apartment above, which she'd had converted into two levels. With shaky hands, she keyed in the code for her private elevator, and as it whisked her up to the second floor, she used those precious seconds to regain her breath.

She had a contingency plan of sorts, had long ago strategized what she needed to do should her secret be discovered. It was simple and yet complex. She had to disappear. Permanently.

She flicked on a light. It seemed too bright suddenly, like a flare attracting the enemy. But she couldn't sweat on the small stuff now. She didn't have her father's uncanny gargoyle eyesight, nor his superior hearing and sense of smell. She had to rely solely on her human senses.

On unsteady legs she moved through the huge, slate-tiled sitting room that dominated the lower floor, and past her expansive stainless steel kitchen. This once she didn't take in the sweeping views of the city lights through double-glazed windows, didn't appreciate the handpicked décor that was an eclectic mix of custom-made and flea market buys.

She paused only when she'd gained the foot of the staircase leading to her bedroom and study, her heart wrenching at Pascal's—Yve's—gargoyle figurine, which guarded the only access to upstairs. She reached out, then quickly pulled back her hand. Out of all her worldly possessions, she'd miss this exquisite piece of art the most.

Fool! She wasn't about to become sentimental now. Not when her artist lover had set her up for a fall. She took the stairs two at a time, shaking from a betrayal that burned deep inside her soul, feeding anger and grief.

She sucked in a steadying breath. She couldn't dwell on Pascal's deceit. Not now. She didn't have the time to indulge in anything close to self-pity.

Her pulses jerked into double-speed as an alarm screamed into life downstairs.

Here, already?

Chapter Nine

If the would-be kidnappers couldn't quickly decode her elevator, it'd take them no time to break down the triple locked entryway to the stairs—no doubt, with Pascal leading the way.

Pascal.

She shook her head, trying hard not to think about him, about his treachery as she hurried along the wide corridor before darting into her bedroom at the far end. But as she closed the door behind her, all she could imagine—albeit briefly—was her room through Pascal's eyes.

Gossamer wafts of material, like a rainbow of silken harem scarves, hung from her four-poster bed with its black velvet spread. Though unlit, scented candles placed in recessed alcoves along her wall and on top of her dresser, filled the room with vanilla, peach and blossom smells in an enticing bouquet.

Tears blurred her eyes. This was her sanctuary, her haven. But no more. Pascal had seen to that.

She snatched the gold-framed photo off her bedside table, featuring the smiling faces of her mum and dad holding her as a baby. There was no way she'd allow the mobster bastards to see this portrait. Bad enough even one of them might see this private snapshot from her past; worse that those same goons who had seen her dad in his gargoyle form, could as easily put two and two together...

"Damn you, Pascal," she muttered savagely.

Striding past the bed and the erotic images that filled her head despite its scalding aftertaste, she slid open the walk-in robe's double doors. Grabbing a small, bulging backpack from beneath her hanging clothes, she carefully pushed the frame inside.

She froze as wood splintered from one well-aimed kick to the downstairs door. When the next kick sent the door crashing onto the floor, she forced herself to move, cursing under her breath as she slung the backpack over her shoulders before climbing up three shelves attached to the wall of the walk-in robe.

Crouching on a large, overhead ledge, she pushed aside the manhole cover in the ceiling before she carefully hoisted herself through. The approaching tread of some half dozen men up the stairs had her hurriedly pushing the manhole cover back into place.

It took a few seconds for her eyes to adjust to the blackness and make out the crisscross of the beams inside the roof. Then she shuffled slowly, quietly, along the rafters toward a trapdoor she'd had installed when she'd redesigned the warehouse into apartments.

She stilled, closing her eyes for a moment to push back a sudden surge of fear when something crashed just below her. One of the men was searching her walk-in robe.

Opening her eyes, she took a deep breath. She had nothing to fear. Not really. She'd chosen to live here because her apartment was high and perched directly on the edge of an embankment, which steadily receded to a valley of homes below.

Her hated wings were her ticket to freedom.

Minutes later she eased open the trapdoor. She squinted, the first rays of bright, early morning sunlight hitting her eyes, temporarily blinding her.

Shit. She'd left it too late.

Her stomach sank as she edged out onto the eaves. There was no way in hell she'd glide through the air in broad daylight. She'd be hunted like an animal...a beast, if ever word got out that people had sighted a winged human.

The tin roof creaked. Dropping to lunge into a spin, a hand clapped over her mouth from behind, instantly stilling the motion.

"Shh."

Pascal.

She'd recognize that throaty, too seductive voice anywhere. Not to mention his spicy, all-male scent. His mouth so close to her ear sent her now traitorous heart all aflutter, but she jammed the brakes on her all too easily influenced emotions. With something close to self-disgust, she nodded stiffly.

His hand dropped away and she resisted trying to stab him with the pointy end of her elbow before she turned to him and hissed, "Don't touch me, you bastard! Don't you dare touch me!"

"Celeste, I'm not the enemy here."

A window shattered just below them, and as he scanned the rooftop she said, "You expect me to trust you now?"

After everything that's happened.

"Yes. I do."

Her obviously scrambled senses wanted to believe him, even as they urged her to run...to glide. She looked at him hard. "How did you get up on the roof?"

Something thudded behind them—the manhole cover, she realized with a sickening lurch in her belly—when a sharp curse, followed by low snatches of conversation, floated toward them.

He frowned, and then took her hand in his. "I'll explain later. Let's get you to safety first."

She wasn't about to argue now. She followed him to the other side of the flat roof, peering over the eaves to the street below. Pedestrians walked by, cars motored along beside a couple of buses and a taxi. "What, no mattress to land on?" she joked numbly.

He shrugged, his lips curling into a half-smile. "Only in Hollywood."

When the trapdoor crashed opened behind them, Pascal crouched beside a retractable ladder and released the pin from its holding mechanism. The ladder slid free with an audible round of clangs, which echoed across the rooftop.

"Wow, you've really done your research," she said, but her quavering voice gave away her rising tension.

He looked up, his stare shrewd. "I've seen detailed floor plans." His eyes swung over to the wary approach of his father's men. His gaze narrowed. "And one can never be too prepared." He stood, and in one fluid motion pulled her behind him, bringing her arms over his shoulders. "If you value your freedom—hang on."

She'd be a fool not to obey. She tightened her arms around his shoulders and wrapped her legs around his waist. When he took hold of the rungs, wedged his feet hard on the outer legs of the ladder before sliding down as though he was rappelling, she let out a horrified squeak and squeezed her eyes shut.

It was one thing to glide through the air, another to be perched on the back of a man who was almost freefalling, with no inhuman ability whatsoever.

Her lids flipped apart at the sudden jarring impact as he landed on the ground. At the stares of passersby and the loud braking of a car, she muttered feebly, "Perhaps it would've been less obvious to just show them my wings?"

"Hm. Though I doubt my ladder skills would make the front page newspapers." He chuckled darkly. "Your bare ass might though."

She swallowed mortification. She didn't have time to worry about self-pride right now. She slid from his back. When she regained her feet, she swayed, suddenly unbalanced.

"Are you okay?" he asked brusquely.

She nodded, only hazily aware he was hailing a taxi. When one pulled up beside them soon after, he bundled her in before clambering in beside her and giving the driver an address.

Her whole body started to shake, her head running hot then cold.

"You're in shock," he murmured close to her ear. And the next thing she knew he was pulling her close, his arm around her, his warmth seeping into her pores, his self-assurance almost immediately leaching away her distress.

Some five or ten minutes later the taxi had pulled to the side of the road. Pascal paid the driver and then lifted her wordlessly into his arms. He strode at a brisk pace along a narrow suburban street. She hardly noticed the too-large houses on their too-small, manicured lawns. She was too busy breathing in Pascal's unique spicy scent, too busy pressing her cheek against his silken shirt, listening to the strong, steady beat of his heart.

And yet her head warred with her heart. She couldn't possibly trust this man. Could she?

He stopped beside a red Ducati motorcycle and set her gently to her feet. "We don't have much of a head start," he said. Unhooking a helmet dangling from the handlebar, he slipped it over her head before clipping the chinstrap together. With a ghost of a smile he added, "Not yet."

Double-checking her helmet, he asked, "Will you be all right?"

She nodded, her voice muffled when she said, "I'm not so shaky now."

He nodded approval. "All you have to do is hang on and enjoy the ride."

Bare-headed, he swung a leg over the bike. Once he had it roar into life she readjusted her backpack and then climbed up behind him, sinking into his body as she wrapped her arms around him and clung to him like she'd never let go.

She came to understand how deliciously erotic it was to ride pillion wearing no underwear, with the vibration from the motorcycle's powerful engine between her thighs. Add the exhilaration of racing through the Sydney suburbs, the ground a blur beneath them, the warmth of the morning sun whipped away by the still chilly air, the man in front a solid wall of masculinity—and a girl could easily forget about trust and integrity—could easily leave a wet patch on the motorbike seat.

She leaned forward, pressing her face against his flapping silk shirt, allowing that same wind to rip free all her doubts. Pascal was a lot of things. But she felt certain he wasn't cast from the same mold as his father.

Pascal handled the bike with ease, weaving in and out of the traffic as though the goons really were right on their tail. She whooped loudly, turned on, invigorated and scared all at the same time. But she trusted Pascal's ability with the bike. She trusted him, period.

He laughed, the throaty rasp torn away in the wind that now smelled faintly of the sea. She barely noticed. All her thoughts were consumed right then by the fact she trusted Pascal. No explanations. No justifications.

Minutes later Pascal turned the bike into a narrow sealed road and then braked to a stop beside the slatted wall of an old beach house. She pushed away from the intimacy of his body and clambered from the seat, Pascal alighting seconds later with the grace of a well-practiced rider.

She unclipped her helmet and handed it to him. Placing it on the seat he turned back to her, his expression so very somber after the exhilarating ride. "I owe you an explanation."

Waves crashed onto the shore some forty meters away. A seagull shrieked overhead as it soared through the air, and suddenly she ached to share the skies with the bird, glide through the heavens in full sunlight without ever having to worry about someone seeing her.

She blew out a little breath. "Actually, I'd rather not hear an explanation," she said softly. "Not at the moment. I believe in you. And that's enough for now."

He brushed a hand down the side of her face, setting her skin into tingles. "You're amazing, do you know that?" he murmured.

"Even with my wings?" she had to ask.

"Especially with your wings."

Her chest very nearly hurt, an exquisite pain that was a whole different ache from a minute ago. And the cool mask she'd worn for so long slipped even further with his affirmation. "I want you," she whispered. "I want you inside me."

His eyes widened, all possessive and hot. Then he was gathering her close, pulling her against his hard thighs, his even harder cock. His mouth crashed to hers, their lips mashing with urgent demand. He tore his head back, their breaths coming out fast and ragged. Then he was scooping her up, his stare glittering, his face all hard angles and planes.

He strode past the bike and around to the front door, which faced the sea. When he pulled out an old-fashioned key from his pocket and unlocked the door, swinging it open with a bang, she spent little time admiring the quaint, rustic furniture within before his mouth settled onto hers once again, his tongue plunging past her parted lips.

The wall was suddenly behind her and she thrust her arms out of the backpack and let it fall to the floor. His outspread hands cupped her bare ass while she slipped her fingertips beneath his shirt, along the implacable, sinewy strength of his shoulders, down the firm length of his spine with the raised lettering, and then the rippling bands of his abs.

Her pussy twitched, slick with need. And she all but licked her lips as Pascal pulled his mouth from hers.

His shrewd eyes glittering, he unzipped his pants and released his cock. It was hard, thick and primed to explode. And without any preliminaries, any foreplay whatsoever, he drove his hips forward, impaled her with his meat, stretching the walls of her pussy right to the edge of exquisite pain.

"Oh!" She flung her head back, the wall digging into her scalp as she mewled with pleasure-pain. Then he was pulling back, taunting her for a moment when he rotated his hips, the head of his cock probing the entrance between her moist lips.

She was on the verge of begging him not to stop, when he slammed back inside her. She gasped even as he rocked in and out with ever-increasing speed, his eyes never once leaving hers, the cords of his neck standing out in sharp relief.

He dropped her lower and tilted her pelvis up, grinding his cock inside her pussy at a whole different angle. She sucked in a startled breath and, without warning, imploded with an orgasm that had her toes curl and her throat convulse while she groaned release.

Pascal's nostrils flared, his jaw locking tight. A second later he jammed his hips forward, bellowing her name as he came, his seed jetting long and hot inside her.

They were both breathing heavy as she finally untangled her legs from around his waist and dropped onto the hardwood floor. And at the most unlikely moment she put a hand to her mouth and smothered a yawn.

He shook his head and grinned, hooking an arm around her waist before saying throatily, "Time for bed."

Her eyelids drooped and she realized she'd had no sleep the last twenty-four hours. "Will I be safe?" she had to ask.

"Yes. For now."

"For now?" she echoed, her voice husky and thick as treacle with the afterglow of intimacy.

He kissed her brow, his lips tender. "Yes." He drew her toward what appeared to be the only bedroom in the tiny beach house. "This is a friend of a friend's holiday house. I'm guessing we'll have a day, maybe two before my father tracks us down."

"And then?"

"First you need your sleep." He grinned when she threw him a need-to-know look, dropping a kiss then to the tip of her nose before added softly, "Then I have a proposition for you."

Chapter Ten

Celeste woke to the crash of waves on the not too distant shore, the screech of seagulls overhead and an empty space on the bed beside her where Pascal had been.

She stretched, enjoying the bliss stealing over her as she fully awakened. That she felt safe with Pascal was a given. That she felt comfortable around him—along with so many other feelings—leant a lethargy to the satisfaction she'd never once experienced before.

Her belly rumbled as she breathed in the scents of frying bacon, eggs and a waft of toast just done.

Pascal appeared in the doorway, his blue-black hair rumpled and damp from the shower, or perhaps a swim, his chest bare and his long pants riding low on his washboard abs. "You're awake, Sleeping Beauty." He grinned. "I've cooked up some breakfast. And there's orange juice and coffee."

Her mouth watered, but it had little to do with the menu. "Thank you."

Suddenly she felt self-conscious again in a whole new way. Not from her wings, which were still sheathed beneath her dress, but from a connection they now shared between them...an awareness she couldn't deny.

She swallowed hard. "I might have a shower first."

"Of course." He swept an arm toward the door of what was obviously an en suite, and probably the only bathroom in the cabin. "I put a towel on the rail for you earlier, and there's soap, shampoo. Everything you need." Swinging around to return to breakfast duties, he tossed over a shoulder, "I think I'm becoming domesticated. Who'd have thought?"

She couldn't stop the bolt of pleasure surging through her veins at his comment—though she held no expectations they would be lovers for any great length of time. They were each renowned for their single lives.

Pascal liked variety, a different woman for every occasion. She too loved sex, but without the complications of intimacy and touch.

Until now.

She gritted her teeth against the sudden shift of her emotions: hope, need...love.

Love? No! After years of striving to be emotionally barren, she would not succumb to such weakness now. Besides, she'd be nothing short of a fool to expect more between them than what they already had.

She jerked out of bed, desperate to put a stop to her wayward thoughts.

Spying her backpack against the bedroom wall—Pascal must have put it there while she slept—Celeste dragged out underwear, denim shorts and a simple, emerald green t-shirt.

In the cream-tiled en suite with marine feature tiles, she stripped off her clothes before stepping under the hot shower.

She stretched out her wings, sighing with bliss as the water streamed over the bony upper ribs and the fanned out, paper-thin leathery length. She tipped her head back and closed her eyes, allowing the water to spill over her face.

At the sudden tread behind her, she sucked in a startled breath, involuntarily retracting her wings as Pascal joined her in the shower.

"No. Don't do that," he said huskily, stepping behind her. "Please, open your wings."

Warmth suffused her, a slow burn that moved through her veins and sizzled between her thighs, leaving her hot all over. "Okay," she whispered, allowing her wings to fan out, then curling them up and around to fit the eight-foot span inside the shower stall.

"Beautiful," he murmured behind her, reaching out to caress the bony structure of her wings, the tissue-thin webbing.

She closed her eyes, letting out the softest sigh. Every nerve-ending along her wings vibrated in response, came alive under his hands, his touch an intimacy that bordered on sacrosanct.

"What...what about breakfast?" she managed to squeak.

"It can wait." Then he was unclipping her hair, running his hands through the strands and saturating them under the showerhead.

He squeezed out a blob of coconut-scented shampoo and massaged it through her hair, her scalp, his hands kneading and stroking until she couldn't help but let out a groan of bliss. She tilted her head forward to rinse out the shampoo, and then he was tugging her head back gently, lathering her hair with conditioner.

His deft hands not once strayed below her neck, yet her whole body thrummed with pleasure, her nipples sharp points aching for his touch.

Only after she'd rinsed out the conditioner did he move his hands to her front to cup her heavy breasts, his thumb and forefingers stroking her nipples until she wondered if she just might faint with need.

His hands dropped lower still, bracketing her hips. His mouth brushed over her ear. "Are you ready for me?"

Yes. Oh Lord, yes! But right then she couldn't have answered him had her life depended on it.

She saw the glint of his teeth as he knowingly grinned, then he was suckling the sensitive flesh along her throat, his ever-hard cock pushing insistently against her, scraping her back, her buttocks. And suddenly she ached to bent down, expose herself to him fully before thrusting her hips back and sheathing his cock inside her hungry cunt.

Instead, with a desperate mewl she rested her head back against his chest and spread her legs wide, losing herself to the sensation of his forefinger sliding deep inside the channel of her pussy.

"You like that?" he growled possessively. And as she nodded jerkily he sunk another finger deep inside, his thumb rolling over her clit.

"Oh!" she said weakly, grinding against his touch with little involuntary movements that pushed her even closer to the brink of climax.

Abruptly, Pascal spun her around. She sighed, aching with frustration and need.

He cupped her face, watching her with glittering eyes while the shower pummeled around them and steam filled the air. His voice low and husky, he said, "I want to make long, slow love to you." His face grew dark and serious. "I want to make every second amazing."

Suddenly it was her chest that ached. Her eyes blurred and she nodded once again, unable to formulate anything coherent. His adoration stunned her. She could only have been more surprised if he'd said, "I love you."

He shut off the water before opening the steam-fogged glass door and following her through. She stood still as he took his time wringing out her long hair, his hands gentle when the strands snarled and entangled.

He dried the rest of her slowly, pulling the towel back and forth across her ass, her back, then gently smudging the water from her retracted wings, her ankles and thighs until she felt as though she was his most precious possession.

Her lips quivered and then pulled into a cheerless little smile. He might not own her, but he'd managed to take her most cherished commodity.

Her heart.

She released a little breath, content somehow with this life-altering affirmation. Better she faced the facts and dealt with the repercussions head-on, than be crushed by the sudden realization when she watched him walk out of her life.

But then, when his dark head moved forward, his tongue replacing the towel as he licked glistening droplets from the triangle of her pussy, she forgot about everything but the moment.

"Spread your legs," he commanded hoarsely.

Somehow she found the strength to step apart. His hands opened her flesh and his head arrowed to her center. When she felt the touch of his tongue lapping at the sensitized flesh of her clit, sampling it along with the pink flesh of her pussy like she was the most delicious lollipop on two legs, her breath whooshed out on a cry.

She gripped his head and whimpered, "You're going to make me come."

Pascal looked up, his gaze heated, his smile smug. "You want me to stop?"

Resisting the urge to push his head back to where it belonged just then, she whimpered, "No." When he stood, she squeaked, "What are you doing?"

Hooking an arm around her waist, the other behind her knees, he lifted her easily, striding out of the en suite and into the bedroom as he growled, "Finishing what I started." His expression was pure, possessive male. "And this time, no interruptions."

He pressed her onto the bed and she smiled up at him, feeling so gloriously, wonderfully alive. When she pushed her upper torso off the bed, he paused, half-bent over her as she stretched out one of her wings and used the leathery tip to caress beneath his jaw.

Her throat felt thick. Did he have any idea how much this simple act meant to her? "I've wanted to touch you like this...with my wings, for so long now," she admitted.

He pushed his lightly-whiskered jaw into her wingtip, rubbing against her like a sleek, big cat. "You can touch me whenever, however, you want." He turned and pressed a kiss to her wing's filmy skin, and she shivered with the immediate gunshot of pleasure firing through her nerves.

Then he was straddling her, his expression tender but hot as his head lowered, his mouth covering hers, their lips melding, tongues meeting, dancing. With his forearms holding his weight either side of her, she used her hands, her wingtips, to caress the long length of his spine, his supple, corded back and lower, to the firm curve of his ass cheeks.

His cock kicked against her belly, the hard length causing her to squirm with wild, wanton need. He groaned when she broke the kiss to voice hoarsely, "I want your cock in me. I want your hands on me." She gasped as his mouth slid down her neck, his whiskered cheek delicately scraping over her skin. "Please!"

He lifted his head, his amber eyes hard, hot and possessive. "I told you I'd worship your body, make long, beautiful love to you." His mouth quirked into devilish grin as he murmured, "Perhaps later, hmm?"

He didn't impale her in one shock-fulfilling lunge like she anticipated. He tormented her first, the weeping head of his cock brushing between her thighs, scraping her clit, her vulva, and making her moan with urgency before his cock slid ever so slowly inside her.

She spread her thighs wide and then crossed her ankles behind him, pulling him down, driving his cock all the way into her tight heat.

His breath hissed, his facial muscles tightening. Then he lifted his hips and withdrew his cock almost all the way. His eyes flared and he thrust all the way back in, his rhythm smooth and effortless as he rocked in and out, hard and fast. Just the way she craved it.

Her back arched, her nails raking down his back as she came, contracting around his cock, milking it as he exploded inside her with a guttural roar.

Her legs dropped weakly onto the bed. "Wow."

Pascal pressed a kiss to her brow. "I think it's safe to say...we belong together."

She smiled, feeling warm and fuzzy all over, aware for the first time they truly could have a future together. "I think you might be right."

He circled his hips, his half-cocked arousal thickening inside her. "I know I'm right." He pulled out abruptly, and at her startled breath he said huskily, "Breakfast is getting cold." His smile was warm when he leaned down, giving her a lingering kiss. "And as much as I'm ready to fuck you senseless again right now, I'm willing to bet your body isn't."

He was right. She was paying the price from too much of a good thing. Her tender flesh burned from where it was chafed from overuse.

Her lashes swept low, watching as he turned away and dragged on his jocks and his black pants, which he'd left beside the en suite door.

Shirtless, the raised lettering running the length of his spine stood out in sharp relief against his skin, still gleaming from the shower, from their latest bout of lovemaking. It was not a tattoo. The letters appeared to have been branded into his skin. He stilled at the doorway to the dining room-kitchen and asked, "How does breakfast in bed sound?"

She nodded, curious about his brand, yet feeling deliciously lazy and content. "I'd like that."

Five minutes later, they were sharing a plate of over-crispy bacon on limp toast and scrambled eggs that were rubbery, overcooked and cold.

It was the best meal she'd ever had.

She sighed, her head resting on Pascal's shoulder. "I don't think I've ever been happier."

His arm slipped around her shoulders, his artist-roughened fingertips caressing her forearm. "You and me both," he said.

Putting their plate and cutlery onto a side table, he tugged her down beside him on the bed. Facing each other as they lay back, entangled in each other's arms, felt like the most natural thing in the world.

She drank him in. He was beyond good-looking, an incredibly intelligent man with his magnetism enhanced by a hardness lurking beneath the striking veneer.

And he was all hers.

Add the fact she no longer had anything to hide from him, and in that moment she truly felt as if she could walk on air.

She sighed with bliss, running a hand over his smooth chest with its smattering of dark hairs. "Apart from my parents, you're the only person who knows the real me." She tweaked one of his nipples, absently rubbing the puckered ridge. "You have no idea how glad I am we have no secrets."

He stiffened, drawing in a sharp breath.

She bit down on one side of her bottom lip, only too aware of his reaction that had little to do with her touch and all to do with her declaration. Somehow she no longer cared. She was willing to take a risk, tell the whole truth and chance having it all with him...or nothing. "I think I'm falling for you, Pascal."

He paled, his eyes widening even as the sheen in her gaze gave away her adoration. His face visibly tumbled with emotions, one after the other. Then he freed his arm from under her and pushed away from the bed, from her.

Her smile wilted, her face burning. God, she really had put it all on the line, trusted her instincts, trusted him, despite his father's congratulatory words to him on the rooftop. She lifted her chin. She refused to give in to insecurities now, refused to overanalyze his reaction.

"Celeste." He raked a hand through his hair. "You said we have no secrets between us...you're wrong. Very wrong."

Chapter Eleven

Celeste took a slow, steady breath. "Your father?"

He crooked a brow, but his expression was all too serious. "I think it's easier if I...show you."

Her heart sunk to her toes. But she nodded and rocked into a sitting position. About to move off the bed, he lifted a hand.

"No, please. Stay there."

She was trembling, she realized, vacillating between every emotion known and then some. "Okay," she managed.

His stare held hers, his expression somber. "The truth is...I fell for you long ago."

"You did?" she breathed.

"Yes. From the moment I had your father investigated...and saw photos of you."

Investigated? Her heart flip-flopped almost painfully. She swallowed back a hundred questions. There would be a time and place for them later. For now there were more important ones to clarify. "Why me?"

I'm nothing special.

"You captivated me."

She didn't have a reply to that one. Didn't even try to find one once she saw his jaw harden almost unnaturally, his expression freeze before quickly thawing, his whole demeanor shift.

His eyes lit up from within, glowed with animalistic light. Wild. Feral. Her mouth dropped open as she saw his throat convulse once, twice. Something cracked—his jaw, she realized numbly. His face rippled as his skull enlarged. And then his whole body lurched, his belly contracting, heaving, before his torso and shoulders expanded, his bones grinding and shifting.

Huge bat-like wings sprouted from his upper spine and fanned out.

And suddenly how Pascal came to be on her apartment roof all made sense.

From a great distance her ears rang. Tears slid down her cheeks as she silently wept, but she didn't try to swipe her face dry. If these wet tracks were the only signs to show for her years of mental agony...years she'd believed only she and her father carried the gargoyle gene...years where self-loathing, aloneness and pain for being different, inhuman, winged, had become the norm, then she'd be damned if she'd try to hide them now.

"Sweetheart, don't cry," he muttered, looking awkward now, unsure. But still too damned sexy for her peace of mind. He was like some dark angel with a pure soul that'd been exposed to too much wrong.

"Are there any other secrets I should know?" she asked, gathering the bedcover around her.

"This is pretty much everything." His sigh sounded harsh as he raised his hands and dropped them to his sides. "Only I'm not cursed and don't turn to stone at the rising of the sun. I'm flesh and blood like anyone else."

She abstractedly tugged at a wedge of her long hair, her mind whirling with endless questions. "Does this mean your father is—"

"No. He's not a gargoyle. Saul isn't even my real father."

It clicked then—his acknowledgement of being a bastard. Something stirred deep inside and tugged at her heartstrings. The fact that he wasn't the self-assured man everyone believed him to be, only made her want him more.

"And yes, Saul knows all about me," Pascal added. His expression hardened momentarily. "My mother—his lover, could shape-shift into a gargoyle too. In fact, being a gargoyle was her preference. She loved the freedom her wings gave her, loved gliding through the sky. But it was too risky."

Her tears dried as amazement kicked in, pushing every cell in her body into a high. Holy shit! There were other gargoyles!

"My mother met Saul when I was five years old." His shrug was forced and she could see the pain shadowing his eyes. "She left us a year later, and Saul took me under his wing." He managed a wry smile. "His proverbial wing."

His mother had abandoned him? The idea was almost as incomprehensible as the fact there were other gargoyles out there.

"And now he is as obsessed as I am in finding other gargoyles. It's why he said what he did to me earlier. He truly believes you are the key to finding others of our kind...finding my mother."

"So you didn't set me up?"

He frowned. "No!" he said, and then sighed. "Though clearly my stepfather took advantage of my obsession with gargoyles...with you, and let me do all the footwork."

"But how did he know about me, about my...wings?"

He pushed a hand over his face. "He'd seen you a few times at some of the parties we'd both attended. He would have been a fool not to have noticed my interest in you. And soon after when he discovered the image I'd sculptured of you, saw your wings I'd imagined and carefully crafted..."

He'd made a statue in her image?

"My god," she whispered, bunching the bedcover in her fists. "I can scarcely take it all in." Silence gathered around them for a minute before she acknowledged, "At least he's only after me to seek out your mother. He really must love her."

"It would appear so."

"Do you know where she is?" She gulped in a breath. "Where other gargoyles are?"

"Maybe, on both counts," he said, walking to the window and pulling the blind to stare outside, his dark wings flowing down his back, hiding the raised script along his spine. "There's a clan of gargoyles living in secret somewhere in the inland of Australia."

No. Way.

"Your mother told you this?" she asked, barely able to comprehend, to believe, what he said.

"Yes." Pain thickened his voice. "She was desperate to go back there, but worried about me growing up in such a harsh environment." He shook his head. "She hated watching my initiation, smelling my flesh burn while the elders branded our ancient clan name, Triskellon, into my flesh."

"But you would have been just a child?"

He nodded. "Yes. I was five."

She shuddered. Little wonder the lettering was raised. His skin would have been baby soft when it had been charred. "That must have been hell."

He shrugged. "It's one experience I'll never forget. I'm sure my mum won't either. Little did she realize, growing up with a mobster stepfather was the harshest environment of them all. I saw and did things no child...no adult, should."

"I'm sorry," she whispered, aching all over for him.

"No, don't be sorry." He swung around, his eyes becoming almost tender as the shadows seemingly buried there started to fade. "If I hadn't been left behind, I would never have met you."

Hurt and anger suddenly bubbled up, made the blood boil in the middle of her brow. "Then why didn't you tell me you knew?" she asked with gritted teeth. "Why didn't you tell me who you were? Why deceive me?"

He remained still, but his quivering wings gave away his own taut emotions. "You hate your inhumanness," he said roughly. "There was never reason to believe you'd come to love someone who had more to hide than just a pair of wings."

Her hands clenched, gripping the bedcover. "Yes, I hate my wings—but not how you think! It's what they represent that makes me despise them!"

"And what is that?" he asked, his tone gentling, his face knowing.

"Aloneness!" she burst out, hating that he seemed already to know. Hating that he'd probably guessed long ago. "My wings relegated me to a life of secrets where I hid my body and pined for what other 'normal' humans had. Touching. Intimacy. Children!"

Tears poured down her face now, not just for her, but him too. "All I ever wanted was what my parents had, and no matter how many times I told myself I didn't care, I always did."

Pascal's unearthly yellow eyes glistened too. As she pulled her knees up to her breasts, he said softly, "Can't you see what's right in front of you? Your mother was human, your father a gargoyle shape-shifter." He swung out a hand. "What makes you imagine you can't find that same love with a human? With a gargoyle?"

"I don't know..." She bit her bottom lip as rage drained away, feeling the pain of her sharp teeth but glad of the distraction as her head whirled with possibilities, with wild hope. She swiped at the wetness on her cheeks. "I don't...know."

"Then tell me one thing?" He stalked forward, not quite human now, a powerful creature all but bristling with emotion. "Do you want me enough to live away from mortals? Are you willing to give up everything you know to be with me...to find my clan?"

She pressed her head onto her knees and closed her eyes. To be free from all the trappings of human life, to be able to glide through the heavens without fear of discovery. But most of all—to start a new life with the man—gargoyle, she loved! Did he really think there was any other option?

Her eyes flicked open as she felt his weight depress the bed beside her, his hand stroke the side of her face. She lifted her head, absorbing his touch. "I want to be free." His hand moved to cup under her chin and she added, "I want to meet other gargoyles."

His thumb moved back and forth, causing her voice to rasp. "I want to be with you, wherever that may be."

He drew her toward him, his own voice husky as he said, "I love you."

His kiss was long, tender and straight from the heart. And as his lips moved from hers she whispered, "I love you too."

Want more Winged & Dangerous stories from Mel Teshco...
Red Hot Lover

A hot-blooded gargoyle, Zahlee knows that Steele, her gargoyle lover and leader of the Triskellon clan, is her perfect match in every way. But she burns for just one more touch from Saul, the human lover she left behind so many years ago. The same human she entrusted to raise and care for her son, Pascal—to keep him safe from the dangers of the gargoyle lifestyle.

Steele banishes Zahlee from the Triskellon clan and forces her to return to Saul and extinguish all yearning for her mortal ex. She quickly discovers a renewed lust for the only man she has ever loved. Their chemistry cannot be denied and combusts into a raging wildfire she never wants to end.

Zahlee yearns for happiness with her son and her human lover. A gargoyle must sacrifice much to live in the human world, but is she willing to give up everything for love?

Chapter one of Red Hot Lover

Zahlee sucked in a breath and held her outstretched wings steady. Hot, blustery wind streamed past. Adrenaline burned through her veins, not quite neutralizing the icy shivers of alarm shooting up and down her spine.

The ground blurred just meters beneath her soaring, outstretched body but she was going too fast for touchdown now. She'd pushed her ability to the limit, trusted in her flight instincts to beat her lover at his own daring.

Oh, god. I'm not going to make it.

Then the rocky, arid Australian ground dotted with parched grasses abruptly dropped away. Her dancing shadow disappeared into the vast emptiness of a deep valley below and she sailed high through the air, the treetops a distant green below.

She let loose a discordant, exhilarated laugh that dispersed into the bright midday air as a whole different adrenaline overtook her.

Steele, her gargoyle lover, closed in from behind.

An updraft snatched them high. As they leveled out Zahlee wheeled to the left, back into the updraft that would take her higher still. Steele followed, his webbed wings, slightly larger than her eight-foot wingspan, deftly manipulating the thermal currents.

She closed her eyes for a moment, dizzy not from the ever-shrinking scenery below but the delicious lust ricocheting through her naked body and making her pulse race.

This was living! No clothes. No cares. Just the open sky. And the man—gargoyle—ready to take her.

The wind blew along the crease of her pussy, tightening her nipples harder still. Her long hair that she'd snagged into a topknot, whipped errant, dark curls in front of her face, blinding her to Steele as his big hands locked on to her shoulders.

Her pulse pounding in her ears, she moaned, so turned on his touch alone almost sent her into orgasm.

His wings snapped in the air just above hers as he spread her legs with one muscled, hard thigh. His cock teased the opening of her pussy for just a moment, where nerve endings tingled and throbbed with anticipation.

This was just what she needed—who she needed? Her breath caught on a half sob. She didn't want anyone else but Steele. Certainly not the human lover she'd abandoned so many years ago.

Saul Daniels.

Her belly clenched. She'd promised herself to never think of him again.

Fool. She'd thought of little else.

Steele pulled her back. She gasped as his cock speared deep into her tight, wet cunt. And already close to the edge, she instantly climaxed, crying out as Steele rocked inside her then came right after her, his hot seed shooting deep into her contracting pussy.

Their midair fuck had to be brief. They were losing altitude fast.

Steele's hands clasped her face from behind. Still joined, he angled her head so that his mouth could settle on hers in a swift, hard kiss that stamped her as his in the most fundamental way.

Then his head reared back. She glimpsed the flash of his possessive gaze and something else shadowed beneath—a dark, hidden emotion that sent her senses into overdrive.

Something was wrong.

Her breath hissed as he abruptly disengaged. His hand moved to claim hers as he skimmed through the air beside her, carefully elevating his wings above hers.

A clearing, aptly named "the strip", which the Triskellon clan frequently used to land safely, came into sight.

She sneaked a sideward look at her lover, her belly churning. She was all too aware he wanted the one thing she couldn't give, the only thing.

Her love.

His expression radiated intensity. And though he was a passionate, hot-blooded male, particularly after sex, there was a set hardness to his face this time, a tension along his jawline.

Her heart dropped. It should have been all too easy to love him, indeed, there were plenty of women who did. Only, she couldn't give that part of herself.

It had already been taken.

In unison they folded their wings, their legs dropping vertically underneath. He released her hand as they landed with knees bent and their wingtips meeting before compressing together at the back.

They walked together noiselessly through the towering gums, bunya pines and wattle trees where fierce sunlight barely peeked through the foliage overhead. Unable to take the suffocating silence one second longer, she clasped his forearm and drew him to a stop beside her. "Steele, what's wrong?"

He looked ahead, his nostrils flaring as he echoed, "What's wrong?" He twisted toward her, his waist-length, dark hair swishing across his spine, concealing the word Triskellon that had been seared into his skin. His blue-green eyes burned like the sun glinting on the surface of the deep sea. "I'm in love with a woman who is in love with someone else."

Her breath caught. So things were out in the open. At last.

She couldn't deny his words. She was still in love with Saul no matter how much she tried to deny it. That Steele was obsessed with her wasn't any surprise. She'd seen it in his every longing look, his every tender touch and every fierce mating.

Steele should have been her perfect mate. Not only was he the most powerful member of the Triskellon clan—making him their natural-born leader—he was intelligent, handsome as sin, courageous and loyal.

He could also be controlling, unyielding and more than a little manipulative. In general those were great attributes to possess as gargoyle leader but those very "qualities" had been to Zahlee's detriment. "I...I don't know what to say," she whispered.

"Don't say anything," he rasped. "I know you still want your human."

She shook her head in denial. Steele could never learn the truth. Already his love for her teetered dangerously close to obsession. It would be stupid, reckless, to acknowledge his suspicions. "No! No, I—"

"You screamed his name at the height of orgasm," he growled thickly. "You were thinking of him, not me."

Oh, dear god. She closed her eyes, forcing back a hot flush of fear. "Steele...I'm sorry."

"Don't." His eyes glowed, hot and reproachful. His hands moved to her shoulders, his grip fierce. "Don't dare feel sorry for me." Pride was stamped on his face. "That is the one thing I could not forgive you for."

Zahlee stayed mute and still as he nodded once, then released her and stepped back. Seconds later he turned and melted into the trees, leaving her trembling and alone with her thoughts.

As anxiety receded an icy hand of guilt clutched at her heartstrings. Anyone else would bask in Steele's love, feel fortunate to have such devotion from one so powerful and handsome.

Anyone wasn't her.

She let out a weary, resigned sigh. It was time to forget her human lover once and for all. She only wished, yet again, that she'd never left her son in his care.

She'd lost sleep wondering if maybe she could have protected her son, Pascal, even out here in the vast interior of Australia with the crude rules that governed the Triskellon gargoyles. The human world could be as harsh as the gargoyle edicts, undoubtedly more so by some of Saul's standards.

Guilt slid like toxin through her blood. Her "freedom of the skies" had been bought at great cost. Not only had she lost her only child, she'd given up the love of her life too.

Resolve steeled her spine as she began the long walk back to her Triskellon comrades. She'd made her choice, she'd have to live with that decision and push all regrets aside.

She shivered a little, and rubbed her arms. But she wasn't cold. Though Steele's obsession with her gnawed at her gut like an ulcer, he'd been much more to her than a lover. He'd become her protector, her guardian of sorts after he'd sought retribution in her honor when she'd been too emotionally overwrought to seek it herself.

But nothing could stop the panic attacks that had been left behind, a legacy of her assault.

She bit her lower lip. Yes, she should be counting her blessings Steele loved her, despite her failings as his heart-mate. As for her precious son, he would always be a tangible link to the lover she'd never forget.

A winged shadow flickered across the foliage above, circling a few times overhead until the gargoyle was all but skimming the treetops. Zahlee sucked in a breath. This aerial display was silent communication she was wanted. Urgently.

She broke into a fast run, towards the direction of a small clearing just half a mile ahead. The gargoyle overhead would have little choice but to land there—the clearing she and Steele had used was too far away.

When she broke through the trees and into the grassy patch of land, Lolita, an elder of the Triskellon clan, was waiting, visibly impatient.

"There you are!"

Zahlee frowned. "What happened?"

"Not what. Who."

Her frown deepened. "Lolita, what do you mean?"

The elder stepped forward, brushing back a silver-blonde lock of her hair. "Your son. He's come home."

Her thought processes went completely numb and then sped into double time. Pascal was here! Her pulse jerked as another thought took over. Saul. Was he okay? Had her son come with bad news?

She remained immobile for perhaps a millisecond. Then she spun around, taking off in a sprint to where her son awaited at the Triskellon camp.

Unable to use air currents—the gargoyle clan lived in deep caves high at the top of a mountain range—it took precious hours on foot before she finally arrived at the all too silent site that was cast in shadow, the sun drifting toward the far mountainous horizon.

Steele stepped forward from the cave she shared with him, carrying her clothes. His wings were high behind him, his emotions taut. "You got the news."

"Yes," she whispered. Her stomach churned with emotions she'd reined in all too long as she accepted her loose-fitting tunic and pants. She pulled them on, her wings snapping tight against her spine. "Pascal is home."

The Triskellon clan may have outwardly welcomed Pascal into their lives after he was born, but she'd been all too aware of the undercurrent of distrust toward her son. It had been the fundamental reason why she had left all those years ago.

The flesh-burning initiation, where the elders had seared Triskellon along Pascal's spine at the tender age of five, had been the last straw. Knowing he'd yet to face numerous gargoyle inductions that tested the males' strength, endurance and agility, she'd feared her half-human child wouldn't survive. She'd decided there and then that Pascal should experience life among humans, grow up without the pain and distrust he'd endured as a Triskellon member.

But she'd never intended to fall for a human, whose love for her, for a child who wasn't his own, was all exclusive, his adoration overflowing from an otherwise darkened soul.

In some ways, she understood the gargoyles distrust. Her son might have all the physical genetics of a gargoyle, but he did have a human father—and a depraved human at that.

It was no secret she'd been raped by a park ranger when she'd flown too far out of the Triskellon territory. She'd always held an innocent fascination toward humans, even before Saul. And when she'd seen a campfire, a large human hunched over a crude rotisserie of roasting wild rabbit, she hadn't thought about anything more than hiding her wings.

She'd shifted into human form and stepped naked toward the man.

When she'd stumbled back to the Triskellon camp days later, her bright-eyed innocence had been all but snuffed out, her soul darkened. Steele had taken one look at her and silently left to "take care" of her human rapist.

It had never been discussed again.

Steele nodded. "Tonight we celebrate Pascal's homecoming..." She closed her eyes, incredibly grateful and relieved by Steele's acceptance. "But now, it's my duty to send you back to your human lover."

Her lids flicked open, her eyes going wide. "What?"

"You are free to return to your human. I will take care of Pascal and his lover."

Her emotions went numb again even as her thoughts scrambled one after the other. I won't get to see my son before I leave. I'll see Saul again soon. Pascal brought a lover—but surely not a human?

No human would be tolerated here, not with the secrecy of the Triskellon clan.

"All I ask," Steele continued softly, decisively, "is that you stay with your human until his mortality ends, along with your obsession."

Sharp relief filled her, consumed her, even as desperation sucked at her soul. "I need some time with my son," she breathed. "Please, I haven't even seen him yet." She shook her head. "I can't go. I lost Pascal once, I won't lose him again."

Steele's face could have been carved out of the same rock as the humans' fairytale gargoyles. "You don't have a choice, not anymore. "

"Please, I—"

His wings snapped closed. "You'll have all the time you'll need with Pascal after your mortal is dead and buried."

So this was her punishment for not loving Steele? In the gargoyle world, Steele's word was law. Disobedience meant banishment, or worse.

Sorrow tore through her soul, hatred for the gargoyle leader bubbling up to the surface until even her eyes burned.

Bad enough that Steele had forced her to stay after she'd returned, never once allowing her to go back and see Pascal. Now he was forcing her to leave here—with the same outcome—never to see her son.

At least, not any time soon.

She lifted her chin. She wouldn't give him the satisfaction of being witness to her emotional carnage. Dragging in a breath, she mentally gathered every raw and bleeding sentiment back to where they belonged—away from Steele's shrewd, too arrogant stare.

Her heart iced over. Her voice came out like frost. "What about you?"

His eyes flared, hot and possessive. A muscle jerked to life in his set jaw. "I'll be here. And I'll be waiting."

For your exclusive FREE story: Her Dark Guardian, and where you can find out when my next book is available, as well as other news, cover reveals and more, sign up for my newsletter: https://madmimi.com/signups/121695/join

Check out my website – http://www.melteshco.com/

You can also friend me on Facebook at https://www.facebook.com/mel.teshco

Or my author Facebook page at https://www.facebook.com/MelTeshcoAuthor

And occasionally on Twitter at https://twitter.com/melteshco

Contact me: melteshco@yahoo.com.au

If you enjoy my books I'd be delighted if you would consider leaving a review. This will help other readers find my books ◈

The three book series, Winged & Dangerous is also available HERE[1] as a boxset.

___

1. https://www.amazon.com/dp/B00U7WJ00W

About the Author

Mel Teshco loves to write scorching hot sci-fi and contemporary stories with an occasional paranormal thrown into the mix. Not easy with seven cats, two dogs and a fat black thoroughbred vying for attention, especially when Mel's also busily stuffing around on Facebook. With only one daughter now living at home to feed two minute noodles, she still shakes her head at how she managed to write with three daughters and three stepchildren living under the same roof. Not to mention Mr. Semi-Patient (the one and same husband hoping for early retirement...he's been waiting a few years now.) Clearly anything is possible, even in the real world.

Want more Mel Teshco books?
Science Fiction:
The Virgin Hunt Games:
The Virgin Hunt Games volume 1
The Virgin Hunt Games volume 2
The Virgin Hunt Games volume 3
The Virgin Hunt Games volume 4
The Virgin Hunt Games volume 5
The Virgin Hunt Games volume 6
Dragons of Riddich:
Kadin (prequel - book 1)
Asher (book 2)
Baron (book 3)
Dahlia (book 4)
Wyatt (book 5)
Valor (book 6)
The Queen (book 7)
Alien Fugitives:
Nero (book 1)
Jasper (book 2)
Sienna (book 3)
Damaris (book 4)
Zander (book 5)
Jaire (book 6)
Epello (book 7)
Alien Hunger:
Galactic Burn (book 1)
Galactic Inferno (book 2)
Galactic Flame (book 3)
Coming soon
Galactic Blaze (book 4)
Nightmix:

Lusting the Enemy (book 1)
Abducting the Princess (book 2)
Seducing the Huntress (book 3)
Winged & Dangerous:
Stone Cold Lover (book 1)
Ice Cold Lover (book 2)
Red Hot Lover (book 3)
Winged & Dangerous Box Set (all 3 books in the series)
Dirty Sexy Space continuity with authors Shona Husk and Denise Rossetti:
Yours to Uncover (book 1)
Mine to Serve (book 6)
Ours to Share (book 8)
Awakenings series with Kylie Sheaffe
No Ordinary Gift (book 1)
Believe (book 2)
Homecoming (book 3)
Standalone longer length titles: (50k-100k)
Dimensional
Mutant Unveiled
Shadow Hunter
Existence
Standalone novellas and short stories: (15k-40K)
Identity Shift
Moon Thrall
Blood Chance
Carnal Moon
Contemporary:
Desert Kings Alliance:
The Sheikh's Runaway Bride (book 1)
The Sheikh's Captive Lover (book 2)
The Sheikh's Forbidden Wife (book 3)

The Sheikh's Secret Mistress (book 4)

The Sheikh's Defiant Princess (book 5)

The Sheikh's Fake Fiancée (book 6)

The Sheikh's Royal Widow (book 7)

The VIP Desire Agency

Lady in Red (book 1)

High Class (book 2)

Exclusive (book 3)

Liberated (book 4)

Uninhibited (book 5)

The VIP Desire Agency Boxed Set (all 5 books in the series)

Box sets with authors Christina Phillips & Cathleen Ross

Sheikhs & Billionaires

Taken by the Sheikh

Taken by the Billionaire

Taken by the Desert Sheikh

Resisting the Firefighter

Standalone longer length titles: (50k-100k)

Highest Bid

As I Am

Standalone novellas and short stories: (15k-40K)

Stripped

Clarissa

Camilla

Selena's Bodyguard (also part of the Christmas Assortment Box)\

Anthologies:

Down and Dusty: The Complete Collection

The Christmas Assortment Box

Secret Confessions: Sydney Housewives

Don't miss out!

Visit the website below and you can sign up to receive emails whenever Mel Teshco publishes a new book. There's no charge and no obligation.

https://books2read.com/r/B-A-ZFLB-JWVG

BOOKS 2 READ

Connecting independent readers to independent writers.